Once Upon a Christmas

USA Today Bestselling Author
Denise Devine

A Sweet Christmas Romance

Wild Prairie Rose Books

Once Upon a Christmas
Print Edition
Copyright 2018 by Denise Devine
www.deniseannettedevine.com

Once Upon a Christmas is a work of fiction. Names, characters, and incidents depicted in this book are products of the author's imagination or are used fictitiously. Any resemblance to actual events, locales, organizations, or persons, living or dead, is entirely coincidental and beyond the intent of the author or the publisher. No part of this book may be reproduced or transmitted in any form or by any means, electronic or mechanical, including photocopying, recording, or by any information storage and retrieval system, without permission in writing from the publisher.

No ghostwriters were used in the creation of this book. This work of fiction is 100% the original work of Denise Devine.

ISBN: 978-1-943124-08-4
Published in the United States of America
Wild Prairie Rose Books
Cover Design by Raine English

Want to stay in touch with me? Sign up for my newsletter at http://eepurl.com/csOJZL and received a free romantic suspense short story. You'll be the first to know about my new releases, sales and special events.

Want to find more good authors who write sweet romance? Join my reader group - Happily Ever After Stories. If you like sweet romance and want to be part of a great group that has lots of fun and fantastic parties, visit us at: https://www.facebook.com/groups/HEAstories/.

Chapter 1

October 14th

Ashton Wyatt stepped through the front door of the Ramblin' Rose Tavern and flipped on the lights, grimacing at the sticky cobwebs covering her fingers. She wiped her hand on her jeans as she stared in dismay at what used to be West Loon Bay's most popular honky-tonk. In its heyday, locals and tourists had crammed into the town's oldest saloon every night to drink chilled mugs of beer and line dance to ear-splitting country music. Now, the place echoed an eerie silence, with no trace of its former glory in the plastic cups, empty longneck bottles, and discarded pull-tab tickets littering the grimy, carpeted floor. Faded posters and old neon beer signs hung askew on smoky, windowless walls. Battered, mismatched chairs and tables were scattered aimlessly about the gloomy room.

A sudden scratchiness crept up the back of her throat, making Ashton violently cough. She covered her face with a tissue while waving away a cloud of dust motes floating through the musty air. "Everything smells like mold, old grease, and stale beer," she said to her sister and dabbed at her nose with the tissue. "My allergies are already kicking up a fuss." She raised her water bottle to her lips and drank, but it didn't help much. "This place is a dump. It would take a miracle to transform it back into the successful business it once was."

Ashton's younger sister, Grace, made a slow, 360-degree turn.

The corners of her mouth curved with an enthusiastic smile as her large brown eyes took in every detail of the room. "No, it wouldn't," she replied cheerfully. "All it needs is a good scrubbing with disinfectant and some paint. I think we should go for it."

"Are you crazy?" Ashton sniffled as she looked around, stopping at the pendant lights hanging over the billiard table. They used to be green but now were covered with a thick layer of grime mixed with dust. Half of them weren't working and she wondered whether they needed new bulbs or new wiring. "It would probably cost a small fortune just to bring the building up to code. Never mind the price of redecorating." She coughed again. "Can we go now? My eyes are starting to burn."

Grace flipped her long, thick braid of dark hair behind her back. "What did you expect? It's an old building," she said, ignoring Ashton's eagerness to escape. "Old buildings have dust."

Ashton stepped over a smashed Styrofoam carton and approached the pool table. She leaned against the corner, noting the eight-ball sitting next to a side pocket, ready to drop in at the slightest movement to the table. "Look, I don't drink anymore and you've never started, Grace. We have nothing in common with this place. Neither of us knows a single thing about the bar business much less what it would take to open one."

"So what? We can learn," Grace argued as she brushed a wisp of curly hair from her face. "Aunt Rose didn't know anything about operating the business, either, when she bought the building, but she made it a success for over twenty-five years. She told Mom that if we decided to reopen it, she'd mentor us. She also offered a startup loan to help us out."

Ashton pushed herself away from the table. "That's going to cost her a lot of money! Why is she willing to do this for us?"

Grace wandered around the room, smiling with too much enthusiasm for Ashton's comfort. "I guess she wants to keep the business in the family," Grace said. "Now that she's getting married, she doesn't have any interest in operating it anymore, but she doesn't want to sell it, either."

"Yeah, but how can she afford to shell out so much cash for her wedding *and* to us to start up the bar again?"

Grace rolled her eyes. "Come on, Ashton, it's no secret that Rose is smart when it comes to making money. But, even if she didn't have a dime, Alex would give her the funds if she asked him."

Rose's only child, Alexander Lang, had left town years ago with little cash and a scandal brewing but had recently returned, now a world-famous rock star. He had more than enough money for himself and his mother.

"I don't know." Ashton sighed, unconvinced. "It's such a long shot. I'd have to quit my job immediately and sell my townhouse to move back here."

Grace countered with a wry laugh. "Ash, you're constantly frustrated with your job! You should be happy that Aunt Rose has offered us this opportunity. Now you can quit and go to work for yourself. Isn't that what you've always wanted?"

Yes, but...

Lately, Ashton had been giving a lot of thought to resigning from her executive position at Gepson Affordable Housing Corporation in Minneapolis. Over the last few months, she'd gradually become overwhelmed and emotionally drained by the constant demands of her job. Working for a non-profit housing developer wasn't easy. The low pay and high turnover meant they were always short-staffed, but government bureaucracy and the constant pressure of finding new funding sources contributed the most to employee burnout on the executive level. She knew the time had come to make a career change, but she hadn't planned on something this drastic. Granted, she'd always dreamed of one day starting her own business. Never in her wildest dreams, however, had she imagined herself taking over a small-town beer joint in northern Minnesota and certainly not one in such pathetic condition.

"Besides," Grace continued quietly, interrupting her thoughts, "don't you miss Mom and Dad? You hardly ever come home to visit."

A pang of guilt pierced Ashton's heart. "Of course, I miss them. I just..."

Since high school, Ashton had struggled with her relationship with her parents. During her teenage years, she'd run with a bad crowd and frequently got into trouble, making things difficult for her father, an officer in the West Loon Bay Police Department. In the ten years since she'd graduated, her dad, Bob Wyatt had worked his way up to Chief of Police. Ashton had moved one-hundred-fifty miles away, determined to leave the fishbowl atmosphere of small-town life—and her strained relationship with her parents—behind. She still visited them, but only on major holidays and she never stayed overnight. In the last few years, however, a sense of loneliness and restlessness had begun to shroud her heart, fueling her desire to mend her differences with them and grow close to them again. Sadly, the gap between her and her parents had grown so wide she didn't know how to bridge it.

Grace shrieked. "Oh, my gosh! Did you see that mouse?" She scrambled up on the scarred surface of a small, square table. Grace measured an inch or two over five feet tall and weighed about a hundred pounds soaking wet. Standing on a rickety table in green denim leggings and a long red sweater, she looked more like a frightened Christmas elf than a serious business owner. She pointed toward the billiard area. "It ran over there!"

Ashton checked the corner where the mouse supposedly scurried to escape her sister's frantic screams but didn't see any threatening creatures lurking about. "It's gone. You can come down now." She stifled the urge to laugh at her sister's ridiculous reaction. How could Grace run a workingman's bar and keep rowdy customers in line when she couldn't master her fear of one hapless little rodent?

Then again, Ashton faced a monumental problem herself. "Look, Grace, I do miss Mom and Dad, and I do think about moving back to West Loon Bay, but..."

"But what—what's stopping you?"

8

Ashton glanced around the room again. "I can't just walk away from everything I've accomplished and completely start over on a whim—especially for *this*."

"Hey!" Grace hopped off the table, her tennis shoes echoing a loud thud on the floor. Making a grand sweep of the room with her arm, she said, "*This* is being handed to us as a gift. Okay, it's not pretty, but success is what you make of it. Are you going to play it safe and go back to that employer who doesn't appreciate you, or are you going to take a chance and become a partner with me? Because I don't want to be a pre-school teacher for the rest of my life. I want to do something exciting. I'm going to take Aunt Rose's offer!"

"Not without me!"

Ashton and Grace spun around to find their cousin, Allyson Cramer, standing in the doorway. Allyson's straight blonde hair glistened in the golden October sunshine streaming across the floor. She'd lost weight since last Christmas when Ashton saw her at a family celebration. Her snug-fitting aqua Capri pants and matching print blouse showed off her slim curves.

Ashton's jaw dropped as she admired Allyson's stunning new look, but that didn't change the fact that they rarely got along. Their stubbornness and competitiveness made them too much alike. "What are you doing here? How did you know Aunt Rose wanted us to reopen The Ramblin' Rose?"

Allyson strutted into the room, her silver stilettos padding softly on the carpet. "She told me first! That's how Grace found out. I asked Grace if she wanted to go into business with *me*." Allyson's blue eyes twinkled. The corners of her mouth curved in a mischievous grin, revealing perfect white teeth; the result of braces in middle school. "So, if you want to be part of the team, you'll have to ask me *nicely*."

Ashton's ire rose as she cut a glance at Grace to catch her sister's reaction. As kids, she and Allyson had always been rivals and it appeared that the passage of time had not changed that aspect between them. She gritted her teeth. "You look terrific, Allyson. It's too bad it never occurred to you to lose your attitude as well."

Allyson dropped her black designer purse on a table and laughed. "Oh, come on, Ashton. Get over yourself. I'm kidding!"

Grace joined in the laughter, but she sounded nervous, as though she worried that Ashton thought she and Allyson were scheming behind her back. Grace didn't have a scheming bone in her body. Allyson, on the other hand...

Ashton cleared her worsening throat and took another swig of her water. "So, why did Aunt Rose tell you first?"

"Because I'm her favorite niece," Allyson said matter-of-factly. Her mother, Ruth and Aunt Rose were identical twins. Allyson resembled them so much that most people joked they were triplets. She turned to Grace. "Did you tell Ashton about the startup money?"

Grace nodded. "Of course, I did. We can't reopen the bar without it."

Ashton still found it impossible to believe. "Why is Aunt Rose being so generous?"

"No one offered her a helping hand back in the day when she desperately needed one," Allyson retorted as she wandered over to the mahogany bar. "Everyone turned against her and gossiped about her behind her back because she wouldn't say who had fathered Alex." Allyson ran one manicured finger across the counter and examined the dust on it. "People treated Aunt Rose like an outcast. She told me it only made her more resolute to succeed." Allyson smacked her palms together, shaking the dust off them. "I'm pretty sure she's offering it to us instead of selling it because she's determined to keep her property from ever falling into the hands of anyone who mistreated her."

"I can understand that," Ashton said, remembering the humiliation she'd experienced back in her senior year of high school. Malicious and hurtful gossip had spread about her after her boyfriend, Cole Jacobson had cheated on her with her best friend on prom night. She'd moved away that summer to go to college and escape from the stifling existence of small-town life, never looking back.

Except that lately she *had* been looking back and wondering if she'd done the right thing. At the time, running away from all of her problems had seemed like the easiest thing to do. Looking at it now, she realized she hadn't solved anything.

Grace sighed with frustration. "Look, if the three of us are going to join forces and start up this business, we must agree—today—that we're going to do everything in our power to get along with each other. Otherwise, we're just wasting our time and Aunt Rose's money."

"I haven't agreed to anything yet," Ashton quipped, seriously questioning her ability to see eye to eye on managing any kind of business with Allyson. "I'm not convinced this is a smart career move."

"Suit yourself." Folding her arms, Allyson rested her back against the bar, crossing her feet at her ankles. "Grace and I will carry on without you."

"Hey, I never said I *wouldn't* do it," Ashton blurted, worried about her younger sister jumping into the fray alone. "I said I wasn't convinced I *should*."

"Then we're going to sit down and talk this over like intelligent women!" Grace pulled out two chairs and motioned for both girls to occupy them.

Allyson pulled a couple of tissues from her purse and began to wipe the wooden tabletop as Grace dusted off the seats of the chairs.

Once they sat down, Grace smacked her hand in the center of the table. "The conversation can't begin until we all pledge to work together," she snapped, glaring first at Ashton, then at Allyson. "You guys have never gotten along, but you're adults now, so it's high time you did."

Allyson shrugged. "I have no problem with that."

Grace's brown-eyed gaze zeroed in on Ashton. "What about you?"

"Okay!" Ashton held up her palms. "I can do it if she can."

Grace splayed her fingers on the table. "Then let's do it!"

Ashton placed her hand on top of Grace's, followed by Allyson's hand on top of hers.

"Agreed!" they chanted in unison.

Ashton had no idea what to do next as they pulled their hands away and stared at each other in silence.

Then they all started talking at once.

"The carpet has to go," Grace spouted, wrinkling her nose. "It's *gross*."

"I think we should paint the walls creamy white," Ashton added. "About three coats to cover the rancid cigarette smell and to brighten up the place."

"Yeah," Allyson said, nodding in agreement, "and we should hire someone to install a few windows, too. Bring some natural light in here." She pursed her lips in annoyance as she glanced around. "This place is as dark as a tomb."

Ashton pointed toward the ceiling. "Speaking of lights, we need new fixtures. Half of these don't work."

"We need to remodel the bathrooms, too. They're probably..." Allyson made a face and shuddered.

They all burst out laughing.

Now that they had formed a team, ideas began to flow fast and furious. Grace pulled a pen and a notebook from her purse to jot it all down and by the time she'd finished, they had a "To Do" list of remodeling and redecorating tasks four pages long.

Grace frowned at her notebook. "Where are we going to get the money to tackle all of this?"

Allyson sat back, her golden brows knitting together as she thought for a moment. "I know someone who does excellent work. I'll strike a deal with him to complete the priority items and make him agree to wait for payment until after we open for business."

Ashton did a double-take at the notion of delaying payment to a contractor. What kind of idiot would give them instant, long-term credit simply on Allyson's word? "Are you sure he'll go for that without any strings attached?"

"Of course." Allyson grinned. "He owes me more than a few favors."

Everyone went silent again, absorbing the monumental task they were about to tackle.

Ashton gripped the edges of her chair as the stark reality of the situation took hold. Forming this partnership meant she'd have to sell her townhouse, quit her position at work, and move back to West Loon Bay. In other words, give up every shred of stability and security she'd attained in her life to launch out into the unknown. Could she do it? Did she really *want* to do it? But then...

If I don't, will I spend the rest of my life regretting that I passed up the chance to do something risky and exciting?

She looked at Grace for inspiration. Grace smiled back, seemingly unconcerned about the consequences of failure or embarrassment for themselves and their parents if their business went belly-up.

She stared at Allyson, hoping her cousin would give her some assurance they were making the right decision. Allyson's cool blue eyes didn't show any emotion, but the rigidity in her spine and her silence implied that she, too, had worries about turning this broken-down relic into the thriving business it used to be.

The thought of trying to successfully "fill Aunt Rose's shoes" twisted Ashton's stomach into knots.

Grace stood. "So, we're going ahead with it. All of us."

"All of us," Allyson replied, though the uncharacteristic monotone in her answer made her sound uncertain.

Grace stared at Ashton, waiting for her answer.

Ashton swallowed hard. "All of us."

I can't believe I'm actually going through with this. What am I getting myself into?

Only time would tell.

****

"Hey there."

13

Sawyer Daniels looked up from framing a small storage barn in the lot behind his workshop to see Allyson Cramer sauntering toward him.

They had been good friends for most of their lives, but right now, she was the last person he wanted to see...

"Hey, yourself," he said gruffly. "How's bankruptcy court coming along?"

Her smiling face clouded at the mention of her ill-fated interior design business. "I don't want to talk about that right now. I came to ask you for a favor."

He laughed wryly at her boldness, but it didn't faze him. Allyson's directness and honesty happened to be what he'd always admired the most about her. Lately, however, her inability to pay her bills had become the aspect he *least* admired about her. "Well, it's at the top of *my* conversational list. I still haven't received payment for the last two jobs I did for you and Janeen."

She stepped over a couple of wooden planks, her black patent leather stilettos clicking on the blacktop. "Neither have I—but Janeen owes me a lot more than that. I had no idea how much money she was stealing from the company until our checks started bouncing. I wish I'd never gone into business with her."

For someone who didn't have two nickels to rub together, Allyson sure didn't show it. Her black satin slacks and the silky white top looked new and very expensive. So did that fancy-looking handbag with the initials LV printed all over it. He wondered if she'd given herself a last-minute bonus before throwing in the towel or if she'd maxed out one of her credit cards. He had a feeling she'd reached the limit on all of her accounts.

Lucy, his five-year-old black Labrador mix, ran toward Allyson, wagging her tail.

"Stop!" Allyson stretched out her hands. "You'll get dirt on my pants."

"Lucy, get down!" Sawyer quickly wedged himself between

them before Lucy could put her paws on Allyson's pretty clothes. "Sit!"

Lucy obeyed, looking confused as she whined and thumped her tail.

He stepped over to a faded red Coleman cooler, flipped open the lid, and pulled out two chilled bottles of water. "I'll save you some time trying to sweet-talk me. The answer is no."

She frowned, her lower lip protruding in that cute "pouting" expression she always used whenever she had something up her sleeve. "You don't even know what I want yet."

He handed her a bottle of water. "Doesn't matter; I'm pretty sure you either need something built or your car fixed, but I'm not doing any more favors for you until I get paid the ten thousand you already owe me."

She took the bottle and examined the label, raising her brows at the Walmart logo. "That's what I've come to talk to you about. I'm going to settle up with you."

Sawyer twisted off the cap of his bottle. "*But...*" he replied, purposely making it sound more like a statement than a question. He lifted the container to his lips and took a long swig, never taking his gaze off her as he waited for her to fill in the rest of the sentence.

She displayed a disarming smile. "But you have to do another job for me to get it."

"You've got a lot of nerve, you know that? I told you—" He barely got the words out before he began to choke on his water.

She moved close and smacked him between the shoulder blades. "I mean it, Sawyer. I'm going to pay you back, but you have to help me out or I won't be able to get the money. You want to get paid, don't you?"

Straightening, he screwed the cap on his bottle and set it in a holder on the lid of the cooler. "Of course, I do, but if you don't have any money now, how are you going to pay me when I finish the next job?"

"Because I'm going to get the money very soon." She pulled a couple of webbed lawn chairs into the shade and motioned for him to join her. Brushing off the seat of the nearest one, she gingerly sat down, looking as though she expected the chair to fall apart underneath her. "I'm reopening The Ramblin' Rose."

He burst out laughing. "I expected your idea to be off the wall, but this is—"

"Don't laugh!" She gave him a stubborn look. "I used to tend bar in college. Besides, my Aunt Rose is giving me a loan."

Lucy trotted over to Sawyer's chair and sat next to him, resting her chin on his knee.

"Is that so?" He patted Lucy on the head. "I hope she's lending you enough to pay me back, too."

Allyson set her unopened water bottle on the ground beside her chair. "I have to make some changes to the building before the bar opens. That's where you come in." She reached into her handbag and pulled out a handwritten list. "The items in red are the initial modifications I want you to make. The rest will come later as I can afford it. You'll get compensated incrementally as you complete the project. Once I'm open for business, I'll start paying off the old debt."

Renovating that old structure seemed like a waste of time, but he unfolded the paper and scanned the list anyway.

She set her handbag on the ground and leaned toward him. "Meet me at the bar tomorrow for a walk-through and we'll go over the specifics."

He'd grown up in West Loon Bay but rarely went back there, even though he lived only ten miles south in Summerville. In his misspent youth, he'd done his share of partying at The Ramblin' Rose and giving the local cops a hard time, but when he left town, he'd abandoned his old life—and his drinking buddies. Instead, he'd adopted a homeless dog, started a business, and built a house in an effort to make some sense out of his life. Working at The Ramblin' Rose increased his chances of running into some of his former crowd. He had no interest in renewing old acquaintances, especially Cole Jacobson, the best-friend-turned-traitor who'd stolen his girlfriend right from under his nose—on prom night no less. It hadn't taken him long to get over Brenda Miller, but even after all these years, he still lived with the temptation to punch out Cole's lights for double-crossing him.

Let it go... You're not that person anymore. Besides, what happened turned out to be a blessing in disguise. Brenda wasn't the one for you.

Sawyer refolded the page and handed it back to her. "I'm too busy at the moment. I've got my own customers to keep happy."

She groaned loudly in disappointment. "When can you start then?"

"I've got orders for storage barns and a custom fish house to finish. I'm busy until Thanksgiving," he said, hoping she'd be in a hurry, as usual, and decide to hire someone else.

Instead of backing off, Allyson leaned toward him and gripped his arm. "Sawyer, I planned to open by Thanksgiving. I need you on the job *now*."

Gently, but firmly he pulled his arm away. "I can't. I have commitments."

"In two weeks, then." She glared at him, her jaw stubbornly set. "By that time, I'll have a crew on-site working on the cleanup." When he didn't answer, she began to blink back tears. "Come on, Sawyer. You've got to help me. Best friends always stick together. Didn't I help you back when you were starting your business?"

Even though he had no doubt she'd deliberately manufactured the waterworks for his benefit, it still made him uncomfortable. He had a soft spot for Allyson and knew he always would. Friends since childhood, they were as close as siblings and occasionally squabbled like brother and sister, but neither of them ever held a grudge. Bringing up their life-long friendship and how her interior design company had given him jobs when he first went into business for himself seared his conscience. He couldn't say no.

And she knew it.

He expelled a deep sigh of resignation. "All right, I'll meet you at the bar tomorrow morning at ten o'clock, but I can't start the job until the first of November. For this job, I want half of the money down *in cash* and the rest upon completion. Is that understood?"

Smiling, she grabbed her handbag and sprung from her chair, all traces of her former tears gone. "I'm going to see Aunt Rose right now and tell her I've hired you. I think it would be a good idea if she attended the meeting as well." She kissed him on the cheek. "You're the greatest, Sawyer. Gotta go. Tons of things to do!" She left him wiping her peach lipstick from the rough surface of his jaw with the back of his hand. "I'll call you!" she yelled over her shoulder as she hurried to her car, her long blonde hair billowing behind her. How she could run in those ridiculous shoes was anybody's guess.

Lucy smacked his knee with her paw, reminding him of her presence. "You're so jealous of her," he said, chuckling softly as he rubbed her ears. "Don't worry, sweetie, you're still my number one girl."

Sawyer watched Allyson drive away, wondering if he'd ever meet the right girl for him. He knew all of the women in the area. He'd attended school with most of them and dated many, but no one had ever captured his heart; no one had ever given him the emotional rush he'd experienced with Brenda Miller. Had he missed his chance for happiness or had falling in love with her simply given him a taste of what the real thing could be like?

He truly hoped someday he'd find out.

Chapter 2

November 1st

The Ramblin' Rose buzzed with activity as a dozen enthusiastic volunteers swept up trash, cleaned the interior, scrubbed tables and chairs, and prepped the walls for painting.

Ashton stood next to Grace in the center of the room, observing the work going on around them. With the assistance of a small, but energetic crew, they'd spent the morning scouring the kitchen and dishwashing areas. "Well, Grace, what should we tackle next?"

Grace tapped the floor with the toe of her tennis shoe. "Let's rip up the carpet and drag it outside."

"Okay." Ashton sniffled. "The sooner we get this germ bag out of here, the better it will be for me. My sinuses feel like they're going to blow up."

They went to a far corner of the room, pulled up a section of the carpet, and began to peel it back. Sand covered the rotting planks underneath it. A cloud of musty particles swirled in their faces.

"Wait!" Ashton cried and let go, doubling over in a coughing spell.

"My goodness, girls, what in the world are you doing?"

The sisters turned to find their mother standing behind them. Petite, blonde, and blue-eyed, Robin Wyatt stood a little over five feet tall wearing jeans, a long-sleeved, peach-colored turtleneck, and tennis shoes.

Grace loosened her hold on the carpet and straightened, wiping her hands on her jeans. "We're getting rid of this unhealthy piece of junk."

"Well, don't do it like that." Robin slid her fingers into her jean pocket and pulled out a razor knife she'd used to break down empty boxes. "Here," she said, handing the knife to Grace. "Cut it into strips twelve inches wide then roll up the strips and secure them with tape. We'll stack them outside in the back and decide what to do with them later."

"Okay," Grace said with a smile as she gently lay the carpet back down on the floor. "Thanks, Mom. You always know what to do."

Ashton began coughing again.

"Grace will get started on that," Robin said to Ashton. "You need to get some air."

Ashton made her way to the back door with her mother, anxious to leave the stuffy atmosphere behind her. The unseasonably warm weather had lasted through Halloween. Today, however, dark clouds and northerly winds had ushered in cooler temperatures, signifying an irreversible change in seasons. From now on, she couldn't go outdoors without a jacket.

They slipped into their fleece hoodies and stepped outside. The chilly breeze nipped at Ashton's nose, but the crisp, fresh air filled her lungs, making her feel better right away.

Silence enveloped them as they stood in the walkway of a covered storage area in the rear of the building. Ashton covered her mouth to stifle a yawn. She'd risen early and driven the two-and-a-half-hour trip to West Loon Bay from Minneapolis, arriving at daybreak. Robin had insisted on making a large breakfast for the family before Bob went to work and she and the girls headed over to The Ramblin' Rose.

"I'm glad you've already sold your townhouse," Robin said as she zipped up her jacket. "I hear they're in high demand in the Twin Cities."

"My realtor put it on the market last Monday and he'd received four offers by Tuesday night," Ashton replied proudly. "The buyers got into a bidding war, so I made an extra fifteen thousand dollars on the sale. The closing is set for mid-December."

"That's wonderful!" Robin slipped her arm around Ashton's shoulders and gave her a quick hug. "When are you going to start looking for a place in town? I'm afraid there are very few townhouses around here, but I've been asking around about what is available right now. The peak season for real estate is over for this year and there are some nice dwellings in town being offered at reduced prices. Perhaps Dad could set up an appointment with Jim Torgerson to show you what's available."

Jim "Torgie" Torgerson had been the town's sole realtor and insurance agent for as long as she could remember.

"Sure, Mom," Ashton replied after a slight hesitation. "I definitely want Dad's opinion on anything I decide to buy." She didn't want her lack of enthusiasm to come across as ungrateful, but it didn't matter to her whether she bought a house in West Loon Bay or a neighboring town, just as long as she found the right property. She'd already made up her mind that her new residence would have trees and acreage, a place where a cat and perhaps a dog, as well, could roam freely.

Robin smiled. "In the meantime, you can stay with us. If—if you'd like."

Robin's offer sounded sincere, but they both knew Ashton wouldn't accept it because she valued her privacy and her freedom. Staying under her parents' roof would mean going by her father's stern rules, making her once again feel like an errant teen. That said; she understood why her father had always been a strict parent...

Hanging out with a delinquent crowd in senior high school had sabotaged her grades and ruined her reputation. It had also caused her parents, especially her father, a lot of heartaches, public embarrassment, and endless worry. Looking back, she regretted her actions deeply and wanted to repair her rift with him, but she had no idea how to go about it. Bob Wyatt kept his emotions hidden and his thoughts to himself, making it difficult to communicate with him. She hoped that viewing houses together, and asking his advice before making an offer on a property, would give her the opportunity to find common ground with him and begin to heal their relationship.

"Thanks, Mom, but I've already found a place for the time being. I'm renting a furnished cabin at Peterson's Resort."

Once she'd accepted the offer on her townhouse, Ashton had viewed the virtual tour of Peterson's cabins online and had made all the arrangements in advance. Knowing she'd be moving in later today, she'd stopped by the resort before coming to the bar to meet the Peterson staff and pick up her keys. Most of her possessions had been moved to a secure storage facility in Minneapolis until she bought another house, but for now, she'd packed the interior of her car to the roof with necessities.

"Oh," Robin replied softly. Though she didn't show it, Ashton sensed her loneliness and disappointment. "Well, if you need any help moving in, don't hesitate to ask. I'm always available."

A gust of wind whipped Ashton's hair around her face. She shivered. "Th-thank you…"

"You're cold." Robin opened the back door. "We'd better go back inside."

As soon as she entered the building, Ashton began to sniffle again and decided she'd be better off staying away from anything to do with carpeting. Grace had already started cutting it up and sat on the floor, binding the first strip with industrial tape.

Ashton grabbed a bucket and a pair of nitrile gloves from their supplies to scour the equipment behind the bar. As she filled her bucket with warm water and lemon-scented ammonia, she wondered what Allyson was doing to accomplish her share of the work.

As if on cue, Allyson suddenly appeared wearing sand-colored leggings with matching flats and a sky-blue tunic. She strolled through the bar with a clipboard in her hand and a roll of plans under her arm, checking on the progress of her crew.

What?

Ashton left the sink and stormed across the room. "Why are you dressed like *that*? You're supposed to be helping to get this place in shape."

"I am," Allyson said and held out her clipboard. "I'm the project manager." She turned away. "Attention everybody, the pizzas will be here shortly!"

An enthusiastic cheer rose from the crowd, making Allyson look like the hero of the day.

Ashton shook her head in annoyance and went back to work. Leave it to her cousin to snag the easy job.

"Where is he?" Allyson frowned as she checked her Apple watch. "He said he'd be here by noon and it's almost that time now."

"Who are you talking about?" Ashton asked as she scrubbed the counter. "Joe?" West Loon Bay had only one pizza shop and everyone knew the delivery person. Joe Johnson has been working there all his adult life.

"No, Joe is on his way." Allyson tapped her pen on her clipboard. "I'm waiting for my contractor to show up and get started on the improvements."

Resisting the urge to comment, Ashton merely raised her eyebrows and continued to work. Since Allyson had hired him, *she* could track him down.

She had her arms in the bottle cooler, wiping it out when she heard Allyson's voice elevate several notches. Obviously, the contractor in question had just arrived. Ashton didn't mean to eavesdrop, but the deep, sexy voice that replied to Allyson's excited chatter had a disturbingly familiar ring to it.

Ashton froze as powerful memories surfaced. *No, it couldn't be...*

It had been ten years since she'd seen him walking the halls of West Loon Bay Senior High, but suddenly it seemed like only yesterday. Slowly, deliberately, she raised her head, peeking over the counter to

23

confirm her suspicions. A startled gasp escaped from her lips.

Of all the competent, skilled men in the area, why had Allyson hired *him*?

Tall and broad-shouldered, Sawyer Daniels stood at Allyson's side dressed in black jeans, T-shirt, and leather bomber jacket, towering over her as they unrolled the plans across a table. He hadn't changed much. If anything, his handsome features had matured, making him even more attractive. His glossy kohl hair, thick and unruly, brushed the collar of his coat. The permanent shadow darkening his jaw amplified his edgy, bad-boy look.

Without warning, he looked up and gestured toward the bar area. Before she could turn away, their gazes collided. If discovering each other surprised him as much as it did her, he didn't show it. His cool, confident stare perused her with aloofness as his dark eyes locked into hers. Then he looked down at the plans again, as though dismissing her out of hand.

I don't want anything to do with you, either, she thought, glad he had brushed her off. The last thing she needed was to get involved with someone from her past, especially someone whose notorious reputation in West Loon Bay High School had exceeded hers.

****

Sawyer looked away, so distracted he could barely think. He hadn't seen Bob Wyatt's daughter since high school but didn't have any trouble recognizing one of the prettiest girls who'd ever lived in West Loon Bay. She still wore her rich brown hair long and straight. She still went sparingly on the makeup, though she didn't need much to set off the natural beauty of her soft, creamy skin and prominent green eyes. But most of all, the intensity in her solemn expression still projected that tough *I-could-care-less-what-you-think-of-me* attitude she'd worn like a neon badge in high school.

I'm staying away from that one, he thought as he tried to concentrate on the architectural drawings covering the table. *I've outgrown the party scene. It's a dead-end life.*

24

One of the things he didn't miss from his past was constant trouble with the law. He hadn't had a run-in with Chief Wyatt in years and didn't plan to start now.

"Hey! Are you listening?"

Pulling his thoughts away from the misdeeds of his youth, he turned his attention toward Allyson and the clipboard she held, furiously scribbling notes on it. "What did you say?"

She looked peeved over his inattention. "I *said*, I want you to get started on the front windows today. I want people in town to see that we're changing things and to make them curious about it so we have good attendance at our grand opening."

"Sure," he replied, getting back to business. "I'll get set up right away. My help should be here within a couple of minutes."

However, the pizza delivery van had just arrived. Joe Johnson walked in carrying a half-dozen boxes, replacing the smell of disinfectant with the pungent aroma of sausage, pepperoni, and extra cheese. All work came to a grinding halt as everyone pulled the tables together in a long row and began helping themselves to pizza and Coke.

Sawyer went out to his truck to fetch Lucy and retrieve his phone. When he returned, Allyson had a paper plate filled with crispy slices of hot pizza waiting for him. "Here," she said as she offered him the food. "I figured I'd better grab some for you while it's hot."

"Thanks," he said, accepting the plate. "It smells terrific." He grabbed a Coke from one of the beverage-filled coolers for the volunteers and some napkins, and with Lucy on his heels, took the only chair available—across from Ashton Wyatt.

Ashton stared down at her food as she ate, ignoring him.

He did the same, intending to wolf down his lunch and get right to work. He'd just taken a large bite when his phone rang. His helper, Glen, had developed car trouble on the highway and called to say that he couldn't make it to The Ramblin' Rose today. He had to wait for a tow truck to haul his vehicle to a repair shop.

Disappointed, Sawyer hung up his phone and fed a piece of crust to the dog. "Well, Lucy," he said as he watched her swallow it whole. "It looks like we made the trip for nothing."

"What's the problem?" Allyson stood behind him, looking over his shoulder.

"My helper can't make it. I'll have to start tomorrow. I can't get anyone else to come at the last minute."

"No," Allyson said as she waved her clipboard in the air. "I want you to start today. We have to stay on schedule!"

He stood up. "Look, I need—"

"You want some help?" Allyson pointed across the table. "Ashton can do it."

Ashton looked up, her mouth gaping. "I don't know the first thing about carpentry work. Besides, we have a room full of volunteers. Can't you simply ask one of the guys who are already here?"

"I told everyone they could leave after they had pizza," Allyson argued. "That's how I got so many people to show up and work so hard."

Ashton glared at Sawyer as she shoved her plate away. "I'm not finished cleaning the bar. You two, on the other hand…" She folded her arms and glanced from Allyson to Grace.

"Don't look at me!" Grace piped up. "Mom and I are still working on the carpet."

Ashton's eyes flashed with annoyance, clearly letting Sawyer know how she felt about working with him, but she stood up and gathered up her things. "All right. If no one else is willing to be your gopher, I guess I'm the lucky one. The fresh air will be better for me anyway than working inside."

Don't do me any favors, lady.

"Never mind." Sawyer raised his palms to let her off the hook. "I'll just do what I can today and finish the windows tomorrow when Glen is with me."

"No," Allyson replied stubbornly. "You and Ashton need to make significant progress on it *today*."

She clutched her clipboard and strutted away.

Sawyer stared after her, fuming. *I should have never agreed to take on this job. The money isn't worth all the drama that comes with it...*

He finished his pizza and rose from the table, wondering what the day would bring. He needed someone with strong arms to help him lift the windows and set them in place, not a pixie-sized woman like Ashton. He knew someone in town that he could call to assist him when the time came to set the window if it proved to be too heavy for her to lift, but he simply preferred to come back when he had Glen with him.

He and Ashton worked silently at first, only speaking to each other when necessary as they set up the sawhorses and retrieved Sawyer's tools out of the back of his pickup. Luckily, this area of the building had been remodeled before and the old plaster walls had been replaced with sheetrock. He handled all of the measuring and cutting. Ashton's job included the cleanup as he tore off the siding and cut the opening. She also retrieved tools, lumber, and whatever else he told her to do. She surprised him by handling the situation fast and efficiently without complaining.

People walking by on their way to the café on the corner stopped to pet Lucy and observe their progress, often commenting or asking questions. Sawyer's presence on the street was accomplishing exactly what Allyson had anticipated—raising awareness of the fact that someone had taken over The Ramblin' Rose and that the bar would soon be reopening.

"You're doing a great job," Sawyer told Ashton as he finished framing the opening for the first window. Thankfully, he didn't need to reroute any wiring so they were making good time, despite all of the attention they were getting from the townsfolk. "Thanks for sticking around and helping Allyson."

At first, she looked taken aback. Then she started to laugh. "I'm not one of Allyson's volunteers. I'm one of the bar managers. Grace and I both are." She stared at him in puzzlement. "Didn't Allyson tell you? The three of us are opening The Ramblin' Rose together."

So... you're back in town permanently.

He had the urge to ask her what Chief Wyatt thought of her new business venture but immediately changed his mind. Her father's opinions were none of his business.

Realizing Allyson hadn't divulged basic details to him, he quickly changed the subject. "Do you have any experience running a bar?"

"I just left an executive position in the Twin Cities, so yeah, I have managerial experience and I know what I'm getting into." She shoved her hands into the pockets of her red fleece hoodie and leaned against the pickup. The wind had calmed now, making the first day of November somewhat pleasant, despite the gray skies and cold temps. "We've divided the work into three areas until we can afford to hire people. Allyson has bartending experience so that will be her role. I have serving experience so I will be the wait staff." She winced. "And Grace is going to learn to cook."

He tried to suppress a grin but failed, so instead, he bent down and reached into his Coleman cooler for two chilled cans of Coke. They needed a break anyway. "If you manage your money wisely and don't drink up all of your own stock or serve anyone underage, you'll do fine. Having two other people to fall back on is a terrific idea."

"Well...as long as the three of us can figure out how to get along," she remarked and accepted the Coke, dripping with ice water. "So, what's your story?" The snap and hiss from pulling on the tab interrupted their conversation. The fizzy liquid bubbled up and overflowed onto the sidewalk. "How did you get dragged into our mess?"

He didn't know if Allyson had divulged any information about her bankruptcy woes so he skipped the part about her owing him money. "Allyson and I are old friends," he said simply. "She asked me to do her a favor."

He decided to bring up something that had been on his mind since he'd walked into The Ramblin' Rose, and saw her behind the bar, studying him.

"You've been gone a long time," he stated cautiously, certain she'd let him know if he'd overstepped his bounds. "Why did you come back?"

But she didn't bite his head off. Instead, Ashton pushed herself away from the pickup and stood looking past the old wood and brick buildings and angle-parked cars along Main Street to the water's edge of Lake Tremolo. "I figured it was time."

H-m-m-m... Why now?

"Are you comfortable seeing Cole and Brenda together? They still live here."

She spun around, her long dark hair fanning her shoulders. "Of course, I am. That was ten years ago! I hope people don't think—"

"I don't know what they think." He shrugged. "I live in Summerville now and don't pay attention to what goes on in this town."

"I had a teenage crush on Cole Jacobson." She set her soda can on the lowered tailgate of his pickup and gripped her hands on her hips. "He cheated on me. We broke up. I moved away and got a life. End of story!"

"Whoa," Sawyer replied, surprised at her angry response. "I believe you."

"What about you? Are you comfortable seeing Cole after he stole your girlfriend right out from under your nose?"

"I won't deny I was angry about it for a long time, but I eventually did the same thing you did. I moved away to get on with my life. I rarely see Brenda, and when I do, I'm cordial to her." It had just taken him longer to deal with Cole's duplicity than with losing his girlfriend. Life-long buddies didn't do that to each other...

He thought about that fateful prom night so many years ago. Bob Wyatt had ordered Cole to bring Ashton home by midnight. At about the same time, Brenda had suddenly come down ill and asked Sawyer to take her home as well.

Brenda and Cole secretly met up and spent the night together. Within days, their salacious little tryst had become the hottest gossip around town. The gossip spreading faster than a prairie wildfire proclaimed that Ashton blamed her father's strict rules on Cole's decision to dump her for another girl, but Sawyer had always assigned the blame solely where it belonged—on Cole Jacobson.

He drained the rest of his Coke. "We'd better get back to work if we want to get things wrapped up by dark."

By the time they'd finished installing the first front window, dusk had begun to fall. She and Sawyer carried the sawhorses and his tools inside the building for him and Glen to use the next day. Everyone else had gone home by that time.

"Gosh, I'm so tired, I wish I was at my cabin right now," Ashton said as she walked in the door with the last of Sawyer's equipment and set it on the floor. The clean scent of lemon ammonia filled the air. "I stayed up kind of late last night packing and dragging all of it out to my car. Then I had to get up at four o'clock in the morning to drive up here for breakfast at Mom and Dad's place." She opened the lid on the remaining pizza box and pulled out a cold, congealed wedge of double cheese pizza. "This will have to suffice for dinner because I still have to unpack my car when I get home," she said and ripped off a chunk, tossing it to Lucy. "Grocery shopping will definitely have to wait until tomorrow."

Dark circles under her eyes and the pallor on her face attested to her exhaustion. It concerned him.

"You shouldn't be driving. I'll take you home."

She shook her head. "I can't leave my car here. It's packed full. What if someone broke into it? Besides, I need my shampoo and my coffee pot for tomorrow morning and I don't have any idea where either one is buried in the boxes. I have to bring everything into the house tonight."

He picked up the pizza box and opened the door, waiting for her to shut off the lights and lock up. Lucy followed close behind, wagging her tail. "I'll drive your car."

She grabbed her handbag from behind the bar and fished out her keys. "Then how will you get back here?"

They compromised by agreeing that he would follow her home to make sure she arrived safely.

Ten minutes later, Sawyer drove into Peterson's Resort behind Ashton's car and followed her to the area housing the deluxe cabins. She pulled up to cabin #6, one of the larger units surrounded by tall pines. He had planned to sit in his pickup and watch until she made it safely inside, but changed his mind the moment he saw her fumbling with the lock in the dark. She must have forgotten to switch on the yard light when she checked in to get her key.

"Here, let me do that," he said as he and Lucy arrived at the door. She didn't argue when he pulled the key from her hand. He unlocked the door and turned on the inside light then stood aside, pushing the door all the way open for her to enter. A whiff of pine greeted his nostrils as he peered inside the cozy cabin. The house looked newly remodeled with a knotty pine interior and living room furniture the color of a ripe pumpkin.

"It's cold in here," Ashton said and shivered as she looked around the living room.

Sawyer checked the thermostat and adjusted the setting. "It won't take long to warm up the house."

She collapsed on the sofa with a tired sigh. "I'm not crazy about the color, but this furniture sure is comfortable."

"The furnace just kicked in. Do you mind if I look around a bit? I'll check the windows for you to make sure they're shut tight and locked."

"Sure. Thanks for doing that."

At her tired nod, he went through every room, turning on the lights and checking the windows. "I've never been in one of these deluxe cabins before," he said, glancing around the small kitchen that had been recently remodeled. He scanned the new appliances, cabinets, and countertops. "This one is really nice—"

Ashton sat like a statue on the sofa, fast asleep.

He had a notion to carry her into the bedroom and lay her on the bed so she could get a decent night's sleep, but threw out that idea as soon as it formed in his head. She'd probably wake up and think he was trying to...

Instead, he stacked a couple of throw pillows on one end of the sofa and carefully lowered her down to the cushions. To his surprise, she didn't awaken or even stir. She'd mentioned earlier about unloading her car, but that definitely wouldn't happen now. Unless...

He walked out to her car and opened the passenger door. She'd packed it so full he wondered how she'd managed to drive it from the Twin Cities like that without getting pulled over by the highway patrol for "obstructed view." He began unloading boxes, bags, and clothes baskets filled with her possessions, stacking them in every room throughout the small house. Then he emptied her trunk. One of the boxes contained a multi-colored afghan. He pulled it out and covered her with it.

Bending over her, he swept her hair away from her face to tuck the pretty, crocheted coverlet under her chin. She looked so peaceful, like a slumbering angel with thick, dark lashes hooding her eyes and the delicate widow's peak framing her heart-shaped face. He marveled at how she'd changed from the hot-headed, foul-mouthed girl he remembered to a disciplined, mature woman.

His gaze roamed across her soft, moist lips...kissable lips. Fascinated, he wondered what it would be like to steal a kiss from the sleeping beauty, to savor the taste of her sweet mouth.

He stood up, doubting he would ever find out. It was a tempting thought, but not a viable one. He would never kiss a woman without her permission.

"Come on, Lucy," he whispered as he walked toward the door and turned out the light. Ashton needed her sleep and he had a project in his garage he'd promised to finish tonight for a client. "Let's go home."

Chapter 3

November 2nd

Ashton awoke the next morning, curled up on the sofa, and still wearing her clothes from the day before. Her afghan lay in a heap on the floor.

Where am I? How did I get here?

She pushed herself to a sitting position and groggily stared at the room. The place looked familiar, but she couldn't remember how she got home last night. And right now, she didn't care.

Lying back down, she toed off her tennis shoes and let them drop to the floor with a loud thump. Then she pulled the afghan over her body and went back to sleep.

Sometime later, she awoke again with the sun shining on her face. Blinking furiously, she sat up and looked around. This time she vaguely recalled arriving late last night with Sawyer, but everything after that came up blank.

Sawyer...

He had unlocked the door and let her in.

A stack of boxes lined the wall next to the front door.

How did they get there? Sawyer must have...

She stood up and began to wander slowly through the house, checking out the rooms and making note of where Sawyer had stacked each carton or basket. She desperately wanted a strong cup of steaming coffee but had no idea which box contained her coffeemaker or her coffee. Unfortunately, she didn't have the time to look for them, either.

Speaking of time, where is my phone? I'm probably late.

She found it at the bottom of her purse, completely dead.

Jeez...no coffee, no phone, no clock... I need to get out of here and get some caffeine so I can function.

Luckily, Sawyer had deposited the box with her toiletries in the bathroom. She took a quick shower, found some clean clothes to wear, and left the house. Her first stop was the local café for a huge Styrofoam cup of steaming black coffee before heading to The Ramblin' Rose.

By the time she arrived at the bar, Sawyer had already started working on the second window. Glen, however, was not with him.

"Where's your helper?" she asked as she approached him. Today he had on a worn pair of jeans and a purple Minnesota Vikings sweatshirt.

He picked up his saw and walked toward the building. "The engine in Glen's car blew yesterday so he's busy looking for another vehicle."

She hadn't planned on serving as a carpenter's helper for the second day in a row. Grace needed help with the painting. But she couldn't deny that he'd followed her home out of concern for her safety and took care of things for her so she could get some rest. She needed to return the favor. "If you want my help again, I'll be inside."

His dark brows arched with surprise by her offer. "I just might take you up on that in a few minutes."

She paused with her hand on the doorknob. "Um...thanks for last night. I'll never forget...I mean—" Realizing how that sounded to anyone who might be eavesdropping or passing by, she stopped and looked around, desperate to overcome her embarrassment. Her cheeks began to flame, giving her away.

He smiled mischievously, his eyes twinkling. The cool breeze ruffled his thick hair. "You're welcome."

Thankfully, neither Allyson nor Grace had heard the exchange.

They were sitting on tall stools at the bar, eating fresh cinnamon rolls covered with thick, white frosting.

"It's about time you showed up," Allyson said. "We called, but you didn't answer your phone. Did you get our message?"

"It's dead." Ashton pulled her phone from her purse along with the charger and went behind the bar to plug it in.

"Hmph! That's not very responsible." Grace glared at her in annoyance but continued to eat her breakfast roll.

Ashton bristled at the lecture from her younger sister. "You've got frosting on your face, Grace."

Grace shrugged. "I don't care."

Allyson pushed the box toward her. "Want one? They're from Birdie's Bakery."

Situated directly across the street from the Ramblin' Rose, Birdie's Bakery, one of the town's oldest businesses, had a reputation for the best lefsa and bakery goods in the area. In the morning, the aroma of freshly baked bread wafted along the two-block downtown area known as Main Street, drawing the local merchants to the shop for a cup of strong coffee and their signature item, frosted cinnamon rolls.

After the first bite, Ashton forgot her irritation, lost in the sticky-gooey delight of a morning sugar high.

Allyson handed her a napkin and pointed to a spot of frosting dropped on the bar. "You're painting the kitchen today with Grace."

Ashton shook her head. "I'm helping Sawyer install the other window. What are you doing?"

"I'm sweeping," Allyson replied matter-of-factly.

"Why aren't *you* helping Grace with the painting?"

Allyson made a face, pointing to her hot pink workout suit. "In this?"

Ashton and Grace exchanged glances, rolling their eyes.

The sharp, ear-splitting grinding of Sawyer's electric saw cutting an opening for the next window curtailed further conversation.

Grace cleaned up her crumbs and left to start setting up her painting tools.

Allyson found the broom and began sweeping out the back hallway.

Ashton sipped her coffee and watched Sawyer through the window they had already installed. As he worked, he moved with the confidence of a skilled man who took pride in doing an excellent job. She wondered what had caused him to lose his penchant for carousing and completely turn his life around.

He'd make a good husband for someone. So, after all these years, why is he still single? The question brought her back to her own life. *That's easy for me to ask, but, then again…why am I?*

She'd been so busy building her career, cultivating professional relationships, and establishing her independence with a house, a car, and all of the bills that came with it, she hadn't cared about finding Mr. Right. Now that she'd given up all of that, she realized she'd simply traded one busy life for another. Lots to do, but no one to share it with. The unexpected revelation made her feel profoundly alone.

How does he do it? Or is he really as lonely as I am?

If Sawyer was tired of going it alone, he didn't show it.

****

Toward the end of the day, Ashton's father, Bob Wyatt made an appearance. She had just finished hauling a wheelbarrow of scrap building materials to the dumpster out back and had come into the bar area to get a couple of bottles of water from the beer cooler when her father appeared in uniform at the front door.

Grace stood on a stepladder, painting the wall outside the restrooms when his tall, imposing frame filled the doorway. "Dad!" She climbed down her ladder and ran to him to give him a hug.

Allyson occupied her favorite seat at the bar, talking to a supplier on the phone. She paused for a moment and waved to him to come inside. "Hi, Uncle Bob!"

Chief Wyatt smiled as he wrapped his arms around his youngest daughter, giving her a bear hug. Many people referred to them as "bookends" because Grace's dark hair, brown eyes, and facial features cast her as a miniature of her father. "I just stopped in to see how your little adventure here is coming along."

Though he tried to appear friendly and lighthearted, his gruff voice sounded more like a father lecturing his child than a man having a conversation with one of his adult daughters. Ashton approached him and gave him a quick hug, but the longer she stood in his presence, the more her apprehension grew. She knew he didn't approve of her and Grace operating a bar and he had even tried to dissuade Aunt Rose from encouraging them to get into the business. Through the years, he'd had to deal with too many incidents at The Ramblin' Rose to be comfortable with the thought of his daughters taking it over.

He looked directly at Ashton. "Are you coming for dinner tonight? Your mother is making a pot roast and apple pie."

She nodded woodenly as she stared into his eyes, feeling like he'd just given her a direct order. "I'll be there at four-thirty to set the table for Mom."

"That's good," he said, pinning her with his gaze. "You should give Mom a call and let her know."

"Sure, Dad. I'll call her right away."

She really needed to go back to the cabin and start unpacking, but she didn't want to disappoint her mother. Besides, she knew she'd get a great home-cooked meal and possibly some leftover pie for breakfast tomorrow. Her refrigerator didn't have a single item in it; not even a box of baking soda to keep it fresh.

Her father walked through the bar with Grace at his side, observing the light streaming through the new windows and all of the improvements they had already made simply by cleaning and getting rid of old junk.

"What's going on back there?" Heavy pounding coming from the rear of the building prompted Bob to point toward the area of commotion. Strolling toward the back room, he stopped in the doorway where Sawyer worked ripping out a plaster wall.

Ashton froze, holding her breath. Her father had dealt with Sawyer many times in the past, mostly with Sawyer sitting handcuffed in the back of his cruiser. She wondered if Sawyer had changed in this respect, too, or if he still held deep animosity toward authority figures.

"Well, Mr. Daniels, I'm surprised to see you here. Have you become a business partner with the girls or are you simply helping out?"

Chief Wyatt's booming voice frightened Lucy. She scurried under a nearby table and peered out, watching his every move.

Ashton couldn't see Sawyer's face, but the serious, disciplined tone of his voice spoke volumes as he replied that he had been hired by Allyson to do the work. He described the scope of his project, making his explanation as brief as possible.

She wanted to join in the conversation but warily kept her distance instead. Her father's stony expression clearly showed he hadn't forgotten that she and Sawyer had run with the same delinquent crowd back in the day and she could tell by the rigidity of his stance he had concluded Sawyer's presence meant only one thing; she and Sawyer were "together" as a couple and they were using the bar to revive their old lifestyle. She wanted to explain the truth, but knew it would simply sound to him like an elaborate excuse to cover up her true intentions— something she'd done many times in the past.

"Going to be in town long?" Chief Wyatt's voice held no emotion, but his implied warning came through loud and clear.

"Not any longer than I have to, sir."

Chief Wyatt responded with a curt nod. "Have a good day."

Allyson set her phone on the bar and ran after him as he left the building. "Bye, Uncle Bob!"

Ashton stood in the doorway, watching Bob leave. After his squad car drove away, she approached Sawyer to apologize for finding himself on the receiving end of her father's interrogation tactics.

"Sorry about that," she said to Sawyer as she grabbed her shovel and began to scoop up chunks of plaster from the floor. "It's what happens when your dad is a cop. Every guy who crosses your path gets twenty questions. I know what you're thinking, but I'm used to it—"

He slipped his green pry bar under a wooden lath and paused. "That's not what I'm thinking at all. He's just doing his job."

Stunned by his answer, she didn't know what to say. Instead, she busied herself emptying the contents of the shovel into the wheelbarrow. The plaster dust swirling about the tiny, windowless room filled her lungs and she immediately began to cough.

"Are you all right?" Dropping the pry bar, Sawyer gripped his hands on her upper arms and gently backed her out of the dust-clouded room, his dark eyes wide with concern.

She couldn't answer. Shaking her head, she stumbled out of the building, coughing and gasping for breath. Standing in the covered storage area, she grabbed onto the corner beam to hold herself up as dizziness began to overtake her. She couldn't stay outside long without a jacket, but the need for fresh air took priority over comfort.

Sawyer followed right behind her. "Relax and take a deep breath."

Closing her eyes, she leaned her forehead against the corner post and sucked in the crisp air. Her knees wobbled. "I'm sorry. I can't handle that much dust. My allergies go berserk."

He circled his arm around her waist to support her. "Just lean on me," he murmured, pulling her close. "We'll go back inside when you're feeling better, but I want you to take it easy. All right? I'll clean up the plaster mess myself. I don't want you getting sick."

A chilly breeze swirled around them, causing her to shiver. He repositioned his arm to cover her shoulder, pressing her cheek against the soft fibers of his sweatshirt. "Is that better?"

She nodded, at a loss for words as a whiff of aftershave filled her thoughts, distracting her as she leaned against him. The heat of his arm warming her back and shoulder shot a tingle from the nape of her neck down to her hip but the strength of his hold on her and the resolute tone of his deep voice gave her an innate sense of safety and protection, something she'd never experienced with a man before. She drew in another deep breath, feeling better already.

Allyson appeared at the back door. "What's wrong?" Frowning with concern, she craned her neck to see what they were doing. "Are you okay, Ashton? I heard you coughing your guts out."

Grace appeared behind Allyson. "What's all the fuss about?" Her mouth formed a silent "O" at the sight of Sawyer and Ashton huddled together.

"I got some plaster dust in my lungs," Ashton said quickly as she pulled from Sawyer's embrace and straightened her shirt. "Sawyer was just…helping me stay upright…"

The shocked looks on the faces of her sister and her cousin suggested they saw something completely different and their inquiring minds wanted to know more.

Embarrassed to her toes, Ashton cleared her throat and trudged back into the bar, muttering that they all needed to get back to work. She dismissed the incident and busied herself with another project, but the memory of her cheek resting against Sawyer's broad, muscular chest stayed on her mind all day.

Chapter 4

Later that day…

Allyson disbanded the group early, sending Ashton home with strict orders to get some rest before going to dinner at her parents' house. The idea sounded tempting to Ashton, but she had too much to do to waste the afternoon snoozing on the couch.

She didn't get as much unpacking done as she'd hoped to accomplish before going to dinner at her parents' place. She'd just started putting things away in the kitchen when Grace called.

"Ash, were you sleeping? You should have been here five minutes ago."

"Nope," Ashton said, realizing she'd lost track of time, even though she'd just finished hanging her clock on the kitchen wall. "I'm on my way out the door right now."

She changed into a sparkly red shirt and black denim leggings and left the house.

At dinner, Robin kept the conversation going in her usual bubbly way, but Bob remained stoic, putting the bulk of his attention toward eating his roast beef. Though he rarely shared his thoughts, Ashton knew he had something pressing on his mind but she had no idea whether it concerned his job or his encounter with Sawyer at The Ramblin' Rose.

Knowing Bob's disapproval of their little adventure, everyone tactfully stayed away from the subject of The Ramblin' Rose. Instead, they chatted about Thanksgiving dinner, decorating the house for Christmas, and the December closing on Ashton's townhouse, discussing possible dates for the entire family to view prospective homes with her in January. Robin insisted they make it a family day and have dinner at the Lakeside Steakhouse on Stukey's Bay. Everyone cheered at the idea. It even got a smile out of Bob.

After dessert, Ashton announced she needed to stop by Larsen's Grocery Store before it closed. She thanked Robin for a terrific dinner and left the house with a Tupperware container of apple pie.

She arrived with only a few minutes to spare before the store shut its doors for the day. Crossing items off her list as she pulled them off the shelves, she tossed them into her cart and pushed it quickly down the aisles, hoping to get everything she needed in one trip. The store had very few customers this time of night and she made a mental note to visit Larsen's this late in the evening on a permanent basis.

She stood in the dairy section with a carton in each hand, deciding whether to buy vanilla yogurt or the mixed-berry blend on sale when she heard footsteps approaching her from behind.

"Get the berry flavor. It's better."

Startled, Ashton spun around and found Cole Jacobson's lean, six-foot-four-inch frame towering over her. Dressed in a blue designer polo shirt and khaki pants, the first thing she noticed about him was that he hadn't aged much in ten years. If anything, the passage of time had served him well. He'd grown even more handsome than she remembered. He wore his blond hair shorter now, but the style suited him, making him appear sophisticated and mature.

"I...um..." she replied, staring into his deep blue eyes. "I think I'll get both."

He responded with a generous smile. "It's great to see you again, Ashton." His smooth, deep voice had a profoundly sensual ring to it, as though his lips caressed every word. "You look terrific. How have you been?"

"J-just fine," she replied, becoming uncomfortable at how close he stood next to her, invading too far into her personal space. She took a step backward and bumped into the dairy case. Leaning her arm on her cart, she pushed it slowly, moving along with it. "Grace and I are opening The Ramblin' Rose with Allyson in a couple of weeks so we're in the middle of a major restoration of the building right now."

"I heard about that," he said as he walked along with her. "Somehow, I just can't picture the three of you running a bar together. I remember how much you girls used to fight—"

"How have you been," she asked, changing the subject. "Have your parents retired yet?"

He laughed at the question, but fine tension lines etched the corners of his mouth. "No, my father says he wants to keep working and I'm undecided whether or not it's worth the hassle to manage the place when my parents are still calling the shots. I'm trying to convince them to put it on the market instead."

That sounded about right. As she recalled, he never did like working for his parents because they expected their only son to take his job seriously before they would hand over the reins of their multi-million-dollar operation to him. Selling their thousand-acre resort on Lake Tremolo with an eighteen-hole golf course, a fine arts gallery, and a five-star hotel would make Cole a wealthy man and solve his occupational dilemma. It wouldn't make him a better person, though.

He flashed a megawatt smile. "Why don't you come out to the resort tomorrow afternoon? I'll give you a private tour of the grounds and show you how to practice on the golf simulator. I'll have the chef cater dinner for the two of us in my suite overlooking the resort."

"Dinner with you at the resort?" His bold invitation to entertain her without his wife present threw her off guard and offended her. Just because they had been friends once, didn't mean she wanted to be friends any longer. Especially after the way they'd broken up. Time may have changed his perspective on it, but not *hers*. "I don't think so," she replied warily. "I don't know anything about golf. Smacking a little ball around in the hot sun never appealed much to me. Besides, from what I've heard, you're still married to Brenda." She threw out that last sentence as a jab, letting him know she didn't mess around with married men, especially him.

At the mere mention of his wife, his deep blue eyes hardened, turning icy as he lifted one golden brow. "More or less."

She had no idea what he meant by that, but it didn't matter. She absolutely did not want *anything* to do with him. Period. "No thanks, Cole. I'm really too busy."

When she drew back, he instantly reverted to his smooth, polished demeanor. "What's wrong with a game of golf between old friends? This weather is perfect."

Though the temperature had dropped into the mid-20s, the lack of snow cover kept the course open and a few die-hard souls were still playing every day.

One section of the ceiling lights blinked on and off, notifying customers to bring their purchases to the checkout lanes.

"I need to get going." She swiftly pushed her cart toward the nearest cashier and looked back to see him standing in the center of the aisle with a disgruntled look on his face. "It's been nice seeing you again!" She said it, but she didn't mean it. Years of lecturing by teachers and by her parents to be polite had conditioned her to always say the right thing, even if she didn't feel like it. And she sure didn't feel like being polite to Cole Jacobson.

She stood in line, fighting a sick feeling curling in her stomach at the way Cole tried to come on to her. They hadn't seen each other in ten years! He had a wife! She could care less about having dinner with him or ever speaking to him again.

He's so unlike Sawyer, she thought, comparing the two. Sawyer had dark hair while he was blond. Sawyer had a husky frame whereas Cole was model-thin. Most of all, Sawyer was sensitive and reserved. Cole, on the other hand, acted obnoxiously overt.

Did I really think that? Yes, Cole is obnoxiously overt about his belief that he's irresistible to women...

Sawyer's unruly, collar-length hair looked like he'd combed it with his fingers, but she preferred his dark, rugged appearance and skillful intelligence to Cole's money and obsession for GQ perfection any day. Everything about Cole repulsed her. He was too charming, too friendly...too stuck on himself. And still married to the girl he'd cheated on her with...

She pushed Cole out of her mind and steered her cart up to the cashier, anxious to pay for her goods and leave. As she watched the cashier ring up her groceries, she recognized the woman. "Nellie Berg, how are you?"

"Fine," Nellie replied curtly without looking up.

"It's me, Ashton Wyatt. Don't you remember me?" They had gone through confirmation class together in church.

Nellie looked up, perusing her with raised brows. "Yeah."

Stunned by the woman's coldness, she went silent and took out her checkbook as she waited for the grocery total.

"We *don't* take checks."

Ashton put her checkbook away and pulled out her credit card. Her mother wrote out checks for groceries all the time. Had the store recently instituted a new policy?

She placed the bags in her cart and rolled it through the electric doors just as the lights inside the building shut off. Out in the parking lot, she located her car and pushed the cart over to it to unload her groceries.

Cole sat in the driver's seat of the Mercedes parked next to her Malibu. He pulled the Mercedes around, wedging her cart between the two vehicles. The window in his car door slowly lowered. "Have dinner with me tomorrow night, Ashton. I'll send the limo to pick you up."

"No. I already told you I'm not interested so don't bother me again." She pushed the cart out of the way, jerked open her car door, and began throwing the bags inside. "Go home to your wife, Cole, and leave me alone!"

He said something she couldn't hear and gestured goodbye with a wave, then drove away.

45

Seething with anger, she shoved the rest of her groceries into the car and sped out of the parking lot, vowing never to shop at this store again.

****

November 3rd

Sawyer arrived with Lucy at The Ramblin' Rose before daybreak and let himself in through the back door. He wanted to get the storage closet completely gutted and put up the studs before the drywall crew arrived tomorrow. Since he still hadn't heard from Glen, he'd made a call last night to a local drywall man to help him hang the sheetrock and start the taping phase.

Once the sun came up, he walked down to Birdie's Bakery for a giant cup of coffee and a fresh box of those frosted cinnamon rolls the girls liked so much. The rolls were still warm when he placed the box on the bar and helped himself to the first one.

The girls arrived at nine o'clock, arguing about the cost of their new floor tile as they burst through the front entrance. Ashton and Grace wore old T-shirts and jeans for painting. Allyson walked in wearing a pair of black leggings and a black, sequined top that looked like a very short dress for...doing whatever she did all day.

Okey-doke...

Lucy ran to the door to greet them, wagging her tail.

"Thanks, Sawyer, you're sweet," Allyson said as she opened the box and pulled out one of the rolls.

The rising sun streamed through the new windows, casting golden light across the room and giving the bar an entirely new atmosphere.

"The flooring contractor is scheduled to come in and lay tile this week," Allyson said, giving Ashton and Grace a stern look. "You need to paint the men's room this morning."

Grace made a face.

Allyson gave Grace a sly look. "I'll bet it's the first time you've ever seen the inside of a guy's bathroom."

46

Grace's mouth fell open. "Oh! Like you're such an expert on men's restrooms? Where did you get your experience?"

Ashton began to roar as Allyson and Grace exchanged lively banter.

Sawyer sat at the end of the bar and smiled to himself. Who needed entertainment when he had these three characters to amuse him?

Allyson's phone rang. Snatching it off the bar, she waved her arm for everyone to cease talking. She took the call and wandered around the room as she argued with someone about delivering the new televisions. She wanted to take possession of them as soon as possible to get on the schedule to have them mounted and connected to the local cable channels by Thanksgiving week.

Grace went to set up the ladder and bring her tools into the men's room, insisting they put a yellow sign out front so people didn't use it and mess up the paint.

Sawyer took the barstool next to Ashton and opened the box of rolls, helping himself to another one. Lucy sat at his feet, eagerly waiting for someone to drop something edible on the floor.

He set the sticky roll on a napkin and began to pull it apart, offering her some. "Did you make it to your parents' house for dinner last night?"

"Yeah," she said quietly as she accepted a small piece of his roll. "And I brought home some of Mom's apple pie."

"You seem better today. Did you get some rest?"

She gave him a sideways glance. "No."

"Why not?"

She pursed her lips. "I had to unpack and buy groceries. I can't live on pie."

Something about her answer seemed off. He didn't know of a single woman who turned grumpy at the thought of buying salad and fruit.

"And?"

She glared at him. "And what?"

"I don't know. You tell me."

She stared straight ahead. "I ran into Cole in the store."

Her attitude surprised him a little. And disappointed him—a lot. His thoughts began to flow so fast he didn't realize she was waiting for his response.

She angled her head, giving him a frosty reception. "What's wrong?"

"I thought you were over him," he said quietly.

She looked straight ahead again. "I am, but apparently he isn't over me. Either that or he simply gets a charge out of harassing every new girl in town."

His patience began a slow burn, making him realize his reaction wasn't just because he had a problem with Cole, but because a surge of jealousy had overpowered his ability to think rationally where she was concerned. He placed his hand on her arm, needing to keep her by his side as long as he could. The thought of Cole breathing in her direction, much less touching her, sent a rush of protectiveness through his limbs that he'd never experienced with a woman before. The connection startled her as well and she met his gaze, searching his eyes. He gently squeezed his fingers. "What happened?"

She looked upset, but not with him. "Cole came on to me, right in the store. I mean, thankfully, very few people shop for groceries at closing time, so I don't know if anyone else witnessed it, but he sure didn't seem to care if they did."

Sawyer's fists clenched. "What did he do?"

She gathered her long hair and nervously swept it past her shoulders. "The jerk asked me to meet him in his private suite at the resort for dinner. When I pointed out the fact that he had a wife, he acted like he didn't care, like he didn't want to be married to her any longer."

Sawyer's breath stuck in his throat, but he managed to whisper, "Would you have accepted if he hadn't been married?"

She stared at him, her green eyes flaring. "Of course not! I don't want anything to do with him ever again and I told him so!" She slid off the barstool and stormed away, leaving him feeling like an idiot for upsetting her. But he had to know.

"Ashton, I'm sorry," he said, catching up to her by the kitchen door and placing his hands on her taught shoulders. "I shouldn't have said that," he murmured in her ear so no one else would hear him. "I'm angry at Cole, not you."

"I understand that," she said with a sigh, her shoulders relaxing. "I'm not angry at you, either. I'm upset because Cole waited for me in the parking lot and once he got me alone, he harassed me again."

He stood behind her, breathing in the scent of her—the rich fragrance of shampoo in her hair, the floral perfume in her clothes. Suddenly, he admitted to himself what his heart had been denying since the day he walked into The Ramblin' Rose and caught her beautiful eyes watching him from behind the bar. He wanted more than a working relationship with Ashton Wyatt. He wanted to get close to her and be involved in every aspect of her life.

But first, he needed to make sure Cole Jacobson never bothered her *ever* again.

Chapter 5

Later that afternoon...

"We're done!" Ashton made the last swipe of the bathroom wall with her brush and cheered. "The next time we have to paint this room, we're *paying* someone to do it!"

Allyson walked around the "Caution" sign and peered into the men's room. "You missed a spot."

A chorus of protests erupted, making her laugh loudly. "I'm kidding! Get over yourselves!"

Ashton started collecting their tools as Grace folded the ladder and carried it back to the utility garage behind the building. "When are the tile people showing up?"

Grace had used that term so often she now had everyone saying it.

Allyson checked her Apple watch. "At the end of this week."

The "tile people" were installing a dark, marble-patterned tile in the bar over new subflooring. They were also replacing all of the cracked and broken quarry tiles in the kitchen and dishwashing area. Ashton knew they had to get the work done, but the cost had wiped out the last of their funds. Thank goodness they were opening in a couple of weeks.

Yesterday, they had carried all of the tables and chairs outside to the covered storage area and stacked them before they locked up. Except for the pool table, the bar was empty and every time someone spoke, the person's voice echoed throughout the room.

Working in the back room, Sawyer's heavy-duty framing nail gun sounded like rapid-fire gunshots as he built a framework for the walls of their new storage room.

"Are you just about done in there?" Allyson called to Sawyer. "That noise is driving me crazy."

Sawyer didn't answer. He just kept hammering away with that obnoxious thing.

Someone opened the front door and the rumble of a huge tractor rolling down Main Street echoed through the building like heavy artillery.

Ashton casually turned toward the noise, expecting to see the mailman or one of their suppliers delivering goods. Instead, she froze, her mouth gaping as Brenda Miller-Jacobson advanced toward her, flanked by Nellie Berg, and Brenda's older sister, Marilee. Nellie stood on Brenda's left wearing a dark green ski jacket and jeans. Marilee stood on her right in a black, full-length down coat.

Tall and lithe, Brenda had always projected the graceful image of a ballerina, but she had thinned so much she looked emaciated. Her hip-length fox coat covered most of her frame, but her legs looked like knobby matchsticks under her burgundy leggings. Dark circles underscored her eyes, her hollow cheeks had faded to ghostly white. The only thing still rich and full about her was her shoulder-length copper hair.

"Stay away from my husband," she said in a voice so low it sounded like a hiss. "Don't call him, don't text him, and don't show up at the resort thinking you're going to get past his assistant because she has strict orders to call security if you dare to put one foot on our property. I'm warning you, Ashton. Leave Cole *alone*."

Ashton blinked, so stunned she didn't know what to say. She hadn't seen Brenda in years, but she never thought they'd meet up again like this...

"Why are you threatening me? I don't have the slightest idea what you're talking about."

Nellie exchanged smug glances with Marilee. Then she stepped forward, glowering at Ashton with disdain. "Yes, you do, you lying, scheming little *slut*. I saw you coming on to him last night. You told him you were meeting him for dinner at the resort." She held up her palms and blinked her eyes in a mocking gesture. "It's been nice seeing you again," she said, repeating Ashton's last words to Cole in a sugary, falsetto tone.

"That's ridiculous. I did not!"

"Don't deny it, Ashton. Nellie says everyone in the store heard you." Brenda's amber eyes narrowed. "You think you're clever, but it's obvious to me what your game is. You desperately need capital to fix up this shack you call a building and you think you can convince Cole to give you the cash." She lifted her hand, the one bearing a huge, sparkling diamond—her wedding ring. "But you're not getting your hands on him or *our* money. I can't control where he goes, but I have a lot of friends in this town and they'll be watching *you*."

Ashton faltered, her mind spinning with confusion. Why would Nellie turn against her like this and tell Brenda such lies? Unless…Cole had been unfaithful before and Nellie saw just enough last night to assume…

Perhaps that was why Brenda was so insecure about her marriage she had enlisted friends to spy for her. It added one more reason to the growing list of why she wanted nothing to do with Cole Jacobson. *Ever*.

"That's not true, Brenda," Ashton argued, eager to set the record straight. "I'm not after your husband and I certainly don't need his money. He approached me in the store. I didn't pursue him. I don't want anything to do with him so tell him to leave *me* alone! If he bothers me again, my father will be knocking on your door with a restraining order."

"Don't you dare threaten my husband," Brenda continued, "and don't expect anyone to believe you're the innocent party, either. You've never gotten over the fact that he dumped you and married me instead." She glanced from Nellie to Marilee to let Ashton know they were of one accord and that her long absence had made her an outsider now. "You should have never come back. You don't belong here. If you ever go after Cole again…you'll regret it. I'll make sure of it."

"Shut up, Brenda!" Allyson stomped around the counter and headed toward the women. "You can't barge into *my* bar and start making threats to *my* cousin. If you can't handle your husband," she snapped, pointing an accusing finger in Brenda's face, "that's your fault. But don't blame your failing marriage on someone who's been gone for ten years!"

"Get out," Grace said, chiming in, her eyes glittering as she waved the tip of her paintbrush at Brenda, "and take your posse with you. Get out and don't ever come back! You're not welcome in *here*."

Wow. Go, Allyson. Go, Grace…

Brenda and her cohorts retreated by slamming the door, leaving a tense vacuum in their wake.

Ashton stood with her arms folded, wondering in discouragement what to do now. She'd moved back to West Loon Bay hoping to find peace, not strife, but this nasty little scene could very well mean the beginning of her troubles, not the end.

Sensing someone behind her, she spun around.

Sawyer stood in the back hallway, the grim lines around his mouth indicating he'd witnessed the entire scene. The intense look in his eyes warned her that he intended to take matters into his own hands and do something about it whether she wanted him to or not. Before she could gather her wits and try to convince him not to start any trouble with Cole Jacobson, he'd swiftly turned and walked away. A moment later, the building literally shook as he stormed out the back door.

****

Sawyer jammed his fist into his pocket to grab his keys as he headed out to his truck. He had to find Cole and set him straight before the problem escalated out of control. He'd supervised a few construction projects for Cole's father over the last few years but had purposely kept his conversations with both Jacobson men purely on a professional level.

However, now that Brenda had become involved, the situation had changed. Brenda's show of fear and insecurity where her husband was concerned demonstrated that she was desperate and prepared to fight dirty, if necessary, to force Ashton out of town.

But it had to stop—now.

With Lucy at his side, he jumped into his truck and headed out to Jacobson's Resort. Twenty minutes later, he drove between the stone pillars at the entrance and made his way toward the conference center hotel to find Cole's office.

He left Lucy in the truck and walked into the hotel lobby.

"Mr. Jacobson will see you now," the receptionist informed him after making him wait ten minutes. It had given him time to cool off considerably, but he still intended to have a serious talk with Cole. "His office is on the eighth floor, the first door on the right when you get off the elevator."

Sawyer took the elevator to the eighth floor. He went through the first set of glass doors to a small reception area and encountered another gatekeeper, Cole's assistant. The pretty blonde guided him into Cole's office.

Cole sat between an enormous ornate wooden desk and a room-sized window. The transparent wall provided a panoramic view of the golf course, the art gallery, and the marina on Lake Tremolo. In the summertime, the emerald landscape stretched as far as the eye could see, but now the thick canopy of mature trees was bare, dark silhouettes dotted along the cold, bleak horizon.

"What can I do for you, Sawyer? Are you looking for work?" Cole stood and held out his palm to shake Sawyer's hand, but when Sawyer didn't reciprocate, he pulled it back. "Have a seat."

Sawyer ignored the command.

As soon as the assistant shut the door behind her, Cole's counterfeit smile disappeared. He returned to his chair and stared up at Sawyer, projecting his position of authority.

Sawyer remained standing in front of Cole's desk, staring

pointedly. "Drop the innocent act, Jacobson. You know everything that goes on in this town; that includes where I'm working right now and why I'm here." He leaned forward. "I'm only going to say this once. Keep your hands off of Ashton Wyatt. Don't call her and don't go anywhere near The Ramblin' Rose. If I find out you've harassed her again, we won't be merely talking. Do I make myself clear?"

Cole's unwavering stare relayed his condescension. "It's none of your business who I socialize with whether it be on the street *or* The Ramblin' Rose."

"It *is* when the woman is someone I care for and she doesn't welcome your attention."

"You and Ashton Wyatt?" Cole erupted with laughter. "Dream on, Daniels. She deserves better than a loser like you."

"I may not be rich like you, but I'm happy with my life. I have control over every business decision I make," Sawyer said, taking direct aim at the fact that Cole's parents had a controlling interest in the resort. "And when I get married, I'll never cheat on *my* wife."

"No one starts out that way." Cole's blue eyes hardened, his expression turning to stone. The edge in his voice held a note of bitterness. "But when your wife has dependency issues and all she cares about anymore is that little white slip of paper from her doctor to make sure she gets her daily fix…"

"She threatened Ashton."

Cole gave him a bored look. "Brenda doesn't have either the nerve or the strength to carry it out."

"The two female bodyguards that were with her had plenty to go around."

Cole stood and walked over to the door, swinging it open. "I'll handle her."

On his way out, Sawyer halted in front of Cole, confronting him nose to nose. "You'd better. I'm warning you, Jacobson. Leave Ashton Wyatt alone—both of you—or you'll answer to me."

The door slammed in his face.

Sawyer left the office, determined to keep Ashton safe. Cole Jacobson thought he had gotten in the last word this time, but if he ever bothered Ashton again, no amount of talking would save him from the consequences.

Chapter 6

November 10th

Ashton stared through the window of her car, viewing the white, two-story stucco home with dark brown trim. Growing up, she'd known the original occupants, but because the couple's children were much older than her, she had rarely talked to them in school and had never been inside their house.

Sawyer's friend, Reggie, owned the house now, but it presently stood empty. Reggie had been transferred to Georgia three months prior and had to leave it. According to Sawyer, Reggie had contracted with Jim Torgerson to handle the sale.

She'd arrived a few minutes early and parked in front, taking pictures with her phone as she waited for Sawyer to arrive and show her the interior of the property. Situated at the outskirts of town, the three-bedroom house had a newly-added, three-season porch connecting the garage to the house, a fenced-in backyard, and six acres of open land. According to Sawyer, Reggie had constructed a couple of stalls in the small pole barn behind the house and wired the building for electricity. He and his wife had planned to adopt a pony or two for their kids but never got around to it before his transfer.

Sawyer arrived at their appointed time in his red Dodge pickup and met her at the curb. The large burr oaks surrounding the house were bare now, but their huge limbs, extending like outstretched arms, still looked impressive. West Loon Bay hadn't received more than a trace of snow yet and the ground, covered with frozen leaves, crunched under their feet.

"I talked to both Reg and Torgie this morning," he said as they walked along the sidewalk to the front door. "Torgie has a meeting regarding another property this afternoon, but he said if he's late, it's okay to walk through the house before he gets here. There's a spare key in a magnetic tin under the mailbox."

In the Twin Cities, that arrangement would never fly, but in West Loon Bay, they considered it business as usual...

He found the key under the metal mailbox attached to the house and unlocked the door, leading the way inside. Ashton had expected the room to be chilly, but the interior was pleasantly warm. The front door opened into a small entryway containing a closet and an open stairway to the upper floor. They crossed the entryway to a spacious living room, connected to an adjoining dining room by a broad, arched opening trimmed with dark oak woodwork. Their footsteps echoed on the hardwood floor as they removed their jackets and wandered through the rooms, discussing the details and the meticulous care Reggie and his wife had given the place.

"Even though I've only seen the main floor, I already know I want to buy this house," Ashton said dreamily as she wandered into the dining room and gazed at the crystal chandelier. "I love everything about it, especially the price." Because it had been on the market for so long, the asking price had been reduced. With the equity in her townhome and the extra fifteen grand she'd gained from the bidding war, she estimated her monthly mortgage payment would be half of what she'd been previously paying.

Sawyer flipped the wall switch for the chandelier, flooding the room with sparkling light. "When Torgie gets here, are you going to make an offer on it?"

"I'd love to," Ashton said as she ambled to the kitchen doorway and glanced inside, "but I can't until I close on my townhouse in

December. Right now, I don't have a dime to my name for earnest money. Besides, I need to do a walk-through with my dad before I make an offer. I've already told him I wouldn't make any decisions without seeking his advice first, so I don't want to go back on my word."

Sawyer followed her into the kitchen. "Why don't you ask him to lend you the money? You're not going to need it very long."

She shook her head. "It seems like a no-brainer, I know, but I'm not comfortable asking my parents for money." She glanced up at him. "We haven't been close for a long time. I moved back to West Loon Bay to restart my relationship with them and become part of the family again, but it's going to take some time."

"I'll lend it to you," he said softly.

"Thanks, Sawyer, but I couldn't impose on you like that."

"Sure, you can. Hey," he said, smiling. "I just got a partial payment from Allyson for my work on the building so I'm simply giving you back your own money, anyway."

She laughed. "I'll think about it." Though it was sweet and generous of him to offer, she wanted to handle this all by herself.

She walked over to the built-in china cabinet and opened one of the upper doors made of clear glass panes. "I really like this even though all I have right now is a couple of wine glasses to store in it. Someday, I hope to fill it with beautiful dishes."

They draped their coats over the newel post and took the oak staircase to the second floor to walk through the upper rooms.

In a small bedroom with a sloped ceiling, Ashton paused to gaze out the rear window, fascinated by the view of the sunset. In the distance, the inky black silhouettes of bare trees stood out against a backdrop of fiery gold and crimson light. The dark silhouette of an eagle soared high in the sky as it circled an open area, searching for a meal. "How far does the property go?"

Sawyer stood behind her, looking past her shoulder. "I believe it ends at that line of oaks," he said, pointing to a string of trees far in the background.

She sighed. "I didn't have a view like this from my townhouse. I could only see other houses. And lots of noisy traffic. I've forgotten what it's like to live here. When I walk outside and take a deep breath, the air smells clean and fresh. It's so peaceful here at night and during the day, the pace is much more relaxed than city life. I never realized until now how much I've missed it."

"I could stand here with you and watch the sunset every day. It's precious and so beautiful." He spoke slowly, the air from his lips lightly brushing her lobe. "I'm glad you came back." He stood so close to her that the heat of his body warmed her back. His rough cheek pressed against her hair.

Angling her head slightly, she looked up and saw the sparkle in his eyes. His description hadn't been referring to the view. As their gazes blended, his hands slid around her waist, pulling her close. The power of his strong arms holding her gently against his hard, muscular chest made her pulse surge, yet it also comforted her in a way she'd never experienced before. She instinctively knew she could trust this man with her heart.

He kissed her temple then paused, as though waiting for her response.

"Sawyer," she whispered, wanting him to do it again.

He spun her around, capturing her in his arms. Dipping his head, he pulled her closer as his lips covered hers.

Rising on her tiptoes, she slid her arms around his neck, pressing her mouth into his. She'd wanted him to kiss her ever since that day they were outside together behind The Ramblin' Rose when he'd put his arm around her and held her close to his side.

They stood together, locked in each other's arms, lost in their own private world as the sun disappeared over the horizon and the natural light began to wane.

"The first time I saw you at The Ramblin' Rose, I couldn't believe my eyes," he murmured. "You looked the same, but something about you had changed. You had an air of confidence about you that impressed me."

"The moment I saw you," she replied with an apologetic smile, "I thought you were ignoring me and I got an attitude over it."

He chuckled. "I *was* ignoring you. I figured you were still friends with people from our drinking days and I didn't want to get mixed up with them again."

"Yeah, well that makes two of us," she replied softly. "At first, I assumed you were still hanging out with that bunch, too. I had no idea you'd moved to Summerville. The other day, Allyson told me a lot of those people aren't around anymore. If any of the remaining ones come into the bar to drink I'll be cordial, but they'd better behave themselves or I'll kick them out. They'll be banned from The Ramblin' Rose as long as I own the place."

He laughed. "I don't doubt that. You're spunky like your Aunt Rose."

She raised up on her toes and kissed him to show him she had a softer side to her, too.

He quickly tightened his arms around her, crushing his mouth against hers.

Suddenly, the front door downstairs creaked open. "Hello?" Heavy footsteps pounded on the floor below. "Sawyer? Where are you?"

Surprised, they pulled apart. Ashton had forgotten all about Torgie.

"We're upstairs," Sawyer called out. "We'll be right down."

He slid his hand along the nape of her neck. "That is, right after this..." Drawing her toward him again, he leaned forward and gave her a deep, affectionate kiss.

Not wanting it to end, Ashton curled her fingers around the collar of his flannel shirt, gripping it tightly.

"I wish we could stay right here and take our time," he whispered as he gently pulled her arms from his neck, "but we have to go." He took her by the hand and led her to the top of the stairs.

Jim "Torgie" Torgerson, the town realtor, stood on the bottom step in a long black wool coat, looking up the stairs. When he saw Ashton, he smiled. "Well…" he said in his jolly way, "Ashton Wyatt, how are you? I haven't seen you since you were knee-high riding around in your dad's squad car." His voice, like so many others in West Loon Bay, held traces of a Norwegian accent, the product of growing up in a Scandinavian community. "Sorry, I'm late. I had a meeting with a retired couple to view their house and we got to talking so it lasted longer than I'd intended."

That didn't surprise her. Torgie loved to talk and that quality in him had contributed to his success as a realtor for decades.

The short, gray-haired man removed his sheared lamb hat, stepping aside as they bounded down the stairs and burst into the entryway. "Well, what do you think of the place so far?"

Ashton grinned. "It was love at first sight."

"Have you seen the lower level yet?"

She shook her head. "What's down there?"

"Well, let's take a look." He opened the basement door. "I want you to see the new family room and all of the improvements the owners have made." Torgie caught their joined hands and glanced from Ashton to Sawyer. "Say, you two make a nice couple. Are you getting married?"

His abrupt question rendered them speechless. They stared at each other, absorbing the awkwardness of the moment then burst out laughing.

Chapter 7

November 23rd

"Well, tonight's the night," Allyson said, a hint of giddiness in her voice as she stood behind the bar. "I hope people decide to come here instead of fighting the Black Friday crowd at the mall in Summerville." She wore a pair of black leggings and a long, shimmering top that looked opalescent in the overhead lights. Her long, sleek hair glistened, held behind one ear with a rhinestone clip.

Both Aunt Rose and Aunt Ruth had come early to help string the grand opening decorations and set up the hors d'oeuvres table. The petite, identical twins had their blonde hair styled in long pixie cuts and wore matching dresses—fitted on top, flared on the bottom. Ruth's dress had a peach tint with a gold belt, whereas Rose's dress bore her favorite color, dusty rose, accented with a rhinestone belt.

"Everybody at the beauty salon is talking about the party," Aunt Ruth said in that eager tone of voice she always used when she had some good gossip to share. "They all want to get a look at what you've done to the place."

"Everybody at the beauty salon talks about *everything*, Mom," Allyson countered with a grin. "Where else would the old biddies in this town get their news if they didn't have Trudi Barsness at gossip-central to gather it for them?"

Grace set a cheese tray on the appetizer table among platters of assorted crackers, salsa, and chips. "I hope that means they're coming tonight and bringing their husbands." She glanced at the musicians setting up their equipment on the compact corner stage. "The band cost us a small fortune," she said in a low voice. "It would be nice if we made a decent return on our investment."

Aunt Rose slid gracefully onto a barstool. "I wouldn't worry about it, honey. People in this town never pass up an invitation to a get-together with free appetizers and drink specials."

Ashton and Grace had decided upon a basic uniform of black slacks and a crisp, white oxford shirt. They'd purchased black aprons to wear over their uniforms to make them look official. Grace had paraded around the bar all day, showing off her three-pocket bib apron as she sliced onions and ground hamburger, forming it into patties by hand. Ashton had chosen a classic bistro apron that began at the waist and fell to the tops of her shoes.

Ashton invited Sawyer to be their guest, but after the incident with Cole, he'd announced that for the time being, he intended to fill in as their door security. Starting tonight, he planned to sit at the entrance, with Lucy at his side, and check IDs of all the young people passing through their doors. He knew everyone in town and knew which young people were old enough to drink in the bar, but if anyone from another town showed up, he would need to verify their ages. Ashton wondered if he had learned something about Cole that he hadn't told her, but she couldn't get him to talk about it. He wouldn't say where he had gone the day Brenda marched into the bar, making threats, even though she'd pressed him about it several times.

Oddly enough, no one had heard from Brenda since then.

The bar officially opened at four o'clock, but people began filing in early. By five o'clock, the crowd had swelled to capacity.

Ashton had her hands full waiting on tables and helping Grace. Their simple menu consisted of appetizers, burgers, fries, and sandwiches and they planned to keep it that way until they could hire another cook. She wanted to take a break and spend a couple of minutes hanging out with Sawyer, but she couldn't find the time. Occasionally, she waved to him and kept going.

Chief Wyatt walked in with his wife, Robin on his arm, wearing civilian clothes. Though he looked like an ordinary citizen tonight, he carried himself with the authority of a police chief—solemn and dignified, wary of his surroundings.

Ashton stood nearby, taking a food order when her father arrived. She froze, midway through writing it down as she watched him approach Sawyer.

"Mr. Daniels," he said in his commanding voice, sounding like a police chief. "Are you a regular employee now?"

Sawyer shook hands with him. "I hadn't planned on it, but someone needs to keep an eye on these girls. Might as well be me."

Chief Wyatt stared at Sawyer in amazement.

Ashton, in turn, stared at her dad. Never before in her life had she seen him speechless.

After he and Robin left Sawyer, they made their way to the bar where Allyson served him a craft beer—another first for Ashton. She'd never witnessed her father drink anything but Budweiser in her entire life. Rose and Ruth had invited her parents to sit at a special row of long tables pushed end-to-end that they had decorated for the Mayor and the West Loon Bay City Council.

The party went smoothly all evening. At eight o'clock a local band, "The Boondocks" began to play. Sawyer did a terrific job of overseeing the crowd, but with the police chief and city officials in the room, the guests were on their best behavior.

Toward the end of the evening, Sawyer pulled her aside and hugged her. "How's it going?"

Ashton leaned against him for support. "My feet hurt. I smell like fried onions. And I'm never going to get these grease stains out of my new apron."

He pressed his cheek against her hair and murmured in her ear, "Save the last dance for me, okay?"

The final dance came after the last call for drink orders. As the band announced the closing number, a special request, Sawyer suddenly emerged from the crowd. The singer's voice began to croon the words to an old NSYNC song, "This I Promise You." He took Ashton in his arms and slowly began to guide her around the dance floor.

The soft strains of the melody created a mesmerizing effect. She slid her palms up his chest as her body flowed with the music. "You were the one who set up the band to play this song for us, weren't you?"

He didn't answer; he simply pulled her closer and gazed into her eyes. As they slowly melted into each other, everything else faded away and their world became one with the words to the song.

"I'll always be there for you. I promise," he whispered. "Cole treated you badly, but I'll never let you down."

She rose on her toes and kissed his lips, wanting this moment to last forever. All their lives they'd been friends—from the first grade through the last. Why had they never discovered each other until now? Maybe they'd been chasing the wrong rainbows. Maybe they'd needed to do some painful growing up first. Maybe all of the above.

She kissed him again, aware that every person in the bar was probably watching them, including her parents. She didn't care. She'd fallen head-over-heels for Sawyer Daniels.

And she wanted the whole world to know it.

****

After the bar closed and they'd cleared everyone out, Sawyer took Lucy outside to take care of business and to clean the snow off Ashton's car. The first snowfall of the year had come after dark and had covered everything with six inches of fluffy white powder. He wanted to make sure she had clear windows for the drive home. According to the weatherman, a bitter cold front from Canada was heading their way and the temperature was already starting to drop.

He stepped out the back door, saw the snow, and immediately sensed something was wrong. There were footprints, a lot of them, on the ground around Ashton's car. Suspicious, he walked around the entire vehicle looking for signs of trouble. Other than the prints, he didn't see anything, but that didn't relieve his mind. Something told him he just hadn't discovered it yet.

He cleaned off the windows and brought the dog back into the building.

The girls had finished their closing chores and were sitting at the bar, resting from a long and busy night.

Allyson flashed a mischievous smile. "Hey, everybody, Grace has a new boyfriend."

"I do not!" Grace's face turned three shades of red. "We've just met. We're simply meeting for coffee. I don't think that counts as an official date."

"Get out!" Ashton smacked the counter with her hand. "Who is it? And why didn't you tell me about it first?"

Grace unpinned her long, dark braid and pulled off the ponytail holder, undoing her hair. "There's nothing to tell. Yet."

"Yes, there is," Allyson insisted. "I sent this cute guy from Summerville to the kitchen to complain about his burger being overcooked, but instead of getting a new burger, he got a date with Grace!"

Suddenly, all three girls were talking at once. They went to the storage closet and donned their coats, arguing all the way out the back door about whether or not Grace's date meant she officially had a boyfriend.

Out in the parking lot, Sawyer waited patiently for Ashton to unlock her Malibu. He wanted to make sure her vehicle started before firing up his own.

It didn't start. She kept turning the engine over, but it wouldn't run. And it had an odd chemical smell.

She rolled down her window. "What's wrong with my car?"

He pulled off his red bill cap and scratched his head. "I don't know."

He opened the hood and checked the battery, the fluids, doing what he could without the proper tools, but it didn't make any difference. "We'll have to leave it here for the night," he told her. "I'll come back tomorrow morning and take another look at it."

He brought her home, preoccupied with the possible causes for the engine failure, and making plans to check it out first thing in the morning.

"Hey," he said once he'd pulled up to her cabin, "congratulations on a successful opening. You girls had a nice crowd tonight."

"Thanks," she said with a weary smile. "My feet are killing me."

"Get some rest." He drew close and kissed her. "I'll check on your car in the morning and see what I can figure out. If I can't get it running, I'll pick you up."

"Okay," she said quietly. "I'd better go. I can barely keep my eyes open." She opened the truck door and slowly slid out.

He watched her until she unlocked the door and turned on the living room light, then waved and drove off.

Early the next morning, he went back to The Ramblin' Rose and tried to start her car again. He got the same results, but this time the chemical smell was even stronger. He called a tow truck and had the vehicle towed to Scottie's repair shop in town. Fortunately, he knew Scottie personally and talked the man into putting his best mechanic on the job right away.

After what seemed like an eternity, Scottie himself came into the waiting area, holding a clear sleeve containing the work order. The short, balding man in tan coveralls handed him the paperwork. "I can't tell you what the substance is, but someone dumped some pretty nasty chemical in the gas tank and destroyed the engine of that car."

Sawyer's stomach churned.

Would that someone be associated with Brenda Jacobson, perhaps?

He thanked Scottie, took the paperwork, and drove back to The Ramblin' Rose to search the area for possible clues. On the way, he put in a call to Chief Wyatt to stop by and discuss the damage to Ashton's

Malibu.

"What's the story?" Chief Wyatt asked as Sawyer met him in the parking lot.

"Someone dumped a chemical into the gas tank of Ashton's car and ruined the engine."

Chief Wyatt gripped his hands on his steering wheel and stared out the window of his squad car in disgust. "I knew something like this would happen if she reopened this place. It used to be a magnet for trouble and it still is."

"With all due respect, sir, I disagree," Sawyer said boldly. "This is no random act of vandalism. Whoever did this *knew* what he was doing and he targeted her on purpose. Or she..." Relaying the facts as accurately as he could, Sawyer described the incidents with Cole and Brenda.

Chief Wyatt opened the door of his squad car and got out. "Ashton bought that Malibu new, but she's had it for years and it has high mileage. It's not worth fixing."

Sawyer nodded in agreement as the chief walked around the vehicle and stared at all of the footprints in the snow. "There's a dealer in Summerville who'll buy it for scrap."

The chief got back into his car. "I'll start looking around for another one for her."

Sawyer leaned into the squad car with his palm resting on the top of the door. "Until you catch who is behind the vandalism, I think you should hold off. The next time it could be the brakes. Allyson can pick her up in the morning, but I plan on handling the security here for the time being so I'll take Ashton home at night."

The spark in the chief's eye suggested he had some reservations about that, but he acknowledged it would be for the best.

Sawyer looked him in the eye, determined to gain the man's approval. "You have my word. I'll keep her safe."

Chapter 8

December 1st

Ashton sat at the bar alone, eating the frosting off a cinnamon roll as she waited for Sawyer to answer his phone. Allyson had gone on errands and Grace had called in, indicating she'd overslept and would be late.

"Hey, it's me," Ashton said when he finally picked up the call. "Are you still planning on coming early for lunch? I might be the one cooking it."

"Yeah, I'm leaving right now. Is everything all right?"

"Everything is just *peachy*. Grace called, saying she'll be in late and Allyson left me to do all of Grace's set up work by myself." She sighed. "I'm calling to ask you to stop at the hardware and pick up some salt for the sidewalk."

"I don't know if I'll have time," he said, sounding rushed. "I have to drive to the lumberyard to get supplies for a new job I'm starting this week. Can't Allyson get it?"

"No, she says she has too many errands to do this morning. Besides, she complains whenever she has to haul heavy stuff into the bar. It ruins her shoes."

"Right," he grumbled after a long pause. "We wouldn't want her to ruin her shoes..." He sighed, sounding tired. "Okay, I'll get it for you."

"Thank you! I really appreciate it. Oh, I just thought of something

70

else. Would you mind getting me another string of mini-Christmas lights, too? I'm using them to decorate the stage and I'm a few feet short. I need the twinkle ones, okay? They're on sale. Call me when you get there. I'll have to decide on another color if aren't any more of the multi-colored ones left." Ashton hung up and shoved her phone into her purse, feeling guilty for the never-ending list of favors they asked of him. He'd been working two jobs ever since the bar opened, taking over as their door security at night and running his own business during the day.

She spent a couple of minutes composing her "To-Do" list for the week then slid off the barstool and headed for the storage room to get the new Christmas decorations she'd bought on sale. Sawyer hadn't called back so he must have located another box of the multi-colored twinkle lights. She'd become completely immersed in the holiday spirit and couldn't stop decorating. Even her cabin glowed around the clock from all the lights she'd strung in the windows.

Their business had been slow since the party. The girls had counted on a fair number of local people dropping in for lunch or happy hour, but so far, the crowd had been limited to older patrons who used to hang out with Rose back in The Ramblin' Rose's heyday. The girls didn't know if things would pick up over time or if Brenda's gossip network had damaged their reputation. Hopefully, their current ad in the local paper would draw new people to check out the cheery atmosphere, craft beers, and appetizer specials.

In their new storage room, Ashton grabbed the large plastic bag of decorations and sorted through it, looking for the CDs of classic holiday music she hoped would charm her customers into a festive mood. Slipping one into the CD player, she began to hum along with Bing Crosby's song, "It's Beginning to Look a Lot Like Christmas." As she pulled the lid off a box of ornaments, she heard the hinges creaking on the back door. What an annoying noise. She needed to add that as number 1 to her list of things for Sawyer to fix. They must get a new door that closed properly!

"Allyson, is that you?" She lifted out a glittery ornament and held it up to the light. "You're back kind of early, aren't you? Good, I need help with these decorations before I get started setting up the kitchen."

Allyson didn't answer. At the same time, a cold draft snaked into the storage room, causing Ashton to shiver from the sudden wave of icy air. She set down the box and went out into the hallway between the storage room and the restrooms. The breeze had pushed the back door partially open.

"Jeez, Allyson, it's freezing in here. Next time, make sure you shut this door!" She pushed hard on the door and locked it. Tightening the sash around the waistband of her long chenille sweater, she turned around to head back to her decorating project and screamed, staggering backward as she came face to face with Cole Jacobson.

"You scared me! Don't ever do that to me again!" Shocked to find he had slipped in the back door unannounced, she folded her arms tightly across her chest, unable to shake the sudden chill that had overtaken her, filling her with a sense of caution. "What are you doing here? The bar doesn't open until eleven."

"Is that any way to greet an old friend?" he countered smoothly as his gaze roamed the length of her body.

All of her instincts went on high alert. "What do you want?"

His eyes search hers with unconcealed desire. "You know what I want, Ash. I want *you*."

Fine hairs prickled with goosebumps on the back of her neck.

"I don't recall inviting you here, much less telling you that you were welcome to use the back door any time you felt like it. You're trespassing, Cole. I want you to leave, *now*." She tried to slip around him, but he sidestepped and stretched out both arms, pressing his palms flat against the hallway walls to block her way. "*Let me pass.*"

His golden brows furrowed at her resistance. "We didn't finish our conversation the last time we met." Moving closer, he pulled one hand away from the wall and intertwined his fingers in the silky strands of her hair. "You're more beautiful than ever." He reached out and grasped her chin, stroking her soft skin with his thumb. "I just can't get you out of my mind."

Slapping his hand away, she willed herself to show indifference, even though her heart slammed uncontrollably. She couldn't allow him to sense her fear. "Don't touch me."

"You need someone who knows how a woman like you wants to be touched."

She'd *never* heard him talk in that dark, suggestive tone of voice before. Panic began to well up inside her. "I want you to leave, Cole. Get out now!"

He shifted his balance, pinning her between his body and the wall. In desperation, her hands protectively shot up to his chest and pushed against it.

"I don't want to hurt you," he whispered in her ear as he wrapped his arms around her. "I want to show you how right we are for each other; how great it could be if we were together again."

"Go home to your wife. *She* needs you." She tried to duck under his arm but he held her firm. "Let me *go*."

"I made a mistake, Ashton. What can I say? I should have never gotten involved with Brenda. I should have married *you*." He tried to kiss her, but she turned her head away. "You're strong and smart and ambitious. You should be the woman who sleeps by my side."

"You've made a mistake thinking I'd want anything to do with you," she cried defiantly and pummeled him with her fists. "Leave me alone!"

He pushed her against the wall, sliding his hands up her shirt. "I can't..."

****

Sawyer hung up the phone and stepped into his garage to grab a bag of salt. Instead of driving out of his way to buy that item, he decided he'd give the girls one of his. The Christmas lights could wait until he had time to stop. He tossed the twenty-pound bag of salt in the back of his pickup, and with Lucy in the passenger seat, backed out of the driveway to head for the lumberyard in West Loon Bay.

On the way, his phone buzzed in his shirt pocket. He pulled it out and saw Allyson's name on the screen. At first, he had a mind not to answer it. She probably had a long list of additional items she wanted from the hardware store, but he didn't have time to stop.

The phone buzzed again. He sighed and took the call.

"Hey, Allyson, what's up?"

"Are you going to stop at The Ramblin' Rose? Ashton isn't answering her phone and I need her to call me."

His hands went cold. Something didn't seem right. "Are you sure? I talked to her less than ten minutes ago."

"Yeah, I just tried to call her twice."

That's odd. She would have heard the phone ring and besides, she was waiting for a call back about the lights. Why didn't she answer?

He jumped on the gas pedal. "I'm on my way."

He raced down the highway toward West Loon Bay, keeping an eye out for the local police while he put through a call to Ashton. Worrying about his girlfriend not answering her phone wouldn't fly with the cops as a legitimate excuse for speeding.

Her phone kept ringing until it went to voicemail. He tried again but got the same frustrating results. There could be a very simple explanation for why she didn't answer it. Females, in his experience, were always forgetting to charge their phones, were misplacing them, or accidentally turning off the ringtones. He could find her busy putting up her Christmas decorations when he arrived or...

Screw it...I'll take my chances.

He entered the city limits without slowing down, but not bothering any longer to watch for cops. He needed to get to The Ramblin' Rose *now*. As he flew into the bar's parking lot and slammed on the brakes, the tires on his truck left a trail of rubber across the pavement. His pickup slid to a stop behind the back door.

Leaving Lucy in the truck, Sawyer jumped out just as a squad car rushed down Main Street with its emergency lights flashing. He didn't know if they were looking for him, but he decided not to give them any help. Grabbing the salt bag out of the bed of his pickup, he hoisted it on his shoulder, keeping his face hidden from the squad's view as he swiftly walked to the back door of The Ramblin' Rose and tried to open it.

The handle was locked...

Oh-oh. His heart slammed into overdrive as several possibilities hijacked his imagination. What was going on in there? No one ever locked the back door.

In one swift move, he smashed his shoulder holding the salt sack against the old door, and forced it open. Slivers of wood from the fractured frame flew down the hallway as he burst through like a madman. That which he feared the most had come true. Cole Jacobson had Ashton pinned against the wall...

He stormed in and swung the bag of salt, bashing Cole in the head with such force Cole stumbled backward and landed against the ice machine next to the kitchen door. The bag fell to the floor with a heavy thud, forgotten as Sawyer jumped over it and grabbed Cole by the shirt. Before he could swing, Cole lurched forward and thrust one knee into his stomach. He doubled over with swift pain, distracted long enough for Cole to get away.

The police cruiser screamed to a halt in the back of the building.

Cole stumbled through the barroom to escape by the front door. "You're going to regret this, Daniels!"

Sawyer let him go and dropped to the floor, crawling over to Ashton. She sat with her back to the wall, hugging her knees.

"Are you all right?" Cradling her in his arms, he ignored his own pain and cupped his hand behind her head, pressing her forehead against his cheek. "If he hurt you, I'll—"

"I'm okay," she said with a shaking voice. "Y-you got here just in time. How did you know—"

"Don't worry about that now." He kissed her deeply, relieved to have her in his arms. It felt so good to hold her close. "You're safe and that's all that matters." He tipped her face upward. "I couldn't live with myself if anything happened to you because I love you, Ashton. I love you and I need you."

Her eyes filled with tears.

"Hey," he said softly, "don't cry. I thought you'd be happy."

"I am." She smiled as a sob escaped her lips. "I've been in love with you since the night of the party. When you played that special song for me, I knew you meant every word. No one has ever spoken the words of their heart to me that way before."

"*Mr. Daniels*," Chief Wyatt's booming voice called out as he marched through the back door and glanced around at the splintered mess. "I clocked you going seventy in a thirty-mile-an-hour zone."

Sawyer tightened his grip on Ashton and looked up. "*Not now.*"

Chief Wyatt's sharp eyes took in the scene. "What happened here?"

"Not what," Sawyer shot back, "but *who*. Cole Jacobson just attempted to assault your daughter."

Chapter 9

Ashton curled up on the sofa with a soft blanket and a mug of hot, rich cider. The struggle with Cole had left her with bruises and sore muscles. It had also left her exhausted, both mentally and physically.

At her father's insistence, he and Sawyer had taken her to the emergency room for a checkup to make sure she was as "fine" as she claimed. She'd returned home with a clean bill of health, but with orders from the doctor to take it easy on those sore muscles for a day or two and get plenty of rest.

Sawyer agreed to bring her home, but he wouldn't leave her side. Though the police were trying to track down Cole Jacobson, the man had literally disappeared.

Robin had burst into the emergency room, demanding to see her daughter, and insisted on bringing her home. Amazingly, however, her father had sided with Sawyer, allowing her to go back to her cabin at Peterson's resort. Peterson's had first-class surveillance.

With Lucy curled up at her feet, Ashton leaned back against the pillows and sipped her cider. Though her body had to get some rest, her mind wouldn't slow down long enough to fall asleep.

Sawyer appeared in the living room and sat next to her on the edge of the sofa. He leaned over and kissed her forehead. "How are you feeling, honey?"

She lay back and gazed up at him. "I'm tired but I can't sleep."

"You're too keyed up from the stress." He turned on the television and handed her the remote.

She pulled the blanket to her chin to watch a Hallmark movie and slowly drifted off...

****

December 2nd

The next morning Ashton awoke with more aches than the day before. To make matters worse, her back had stiffened up from lying on the sofa too long and she had a pounding headache.

"I have to get out of here," she complained as she stood and stretched her arms. "I need to get some fresh air."

"No," Sawyer said firmly. "Until Cole is apprehended, you're staying put." He slid his arm around her and pulled her close, kissing her. "I'm not letting you out of my sight."

There has to be somewhere safe that we can go...

"Fine, you can keep your eye on me at my mom's house."

He gave her a grim stare as he shook his head. "No. I promised your father you'd stay out of the public eye and take it easy until you were feeling better. I'll get someone to bring us a box of cinnamon rolls from Birdie's."

She slid her arms around his neck and gazed into his deep brown eyes. He hadn't shaved in twenty-four hours and the rough growth on his lean jaw scraped against her chin. "I'm tired of cinnamon rolls. Come on, Sawyer. It's Sunday. Mom's making my dad a huge breakfast with bacon pancakes. I'm desperate for something to eat that doesn't come out of a box or a can. *Please*?"

She hadn't realized how much good food she'd missed out on in the years she'd avoided visiting her parents, but now that she'd come back, she'd begun to crave her mother's "made from scratch" cooking.

He sighed. "I'll give the chief a call."

At nine o'clock that morning, Sawyer's red Dodge Ram pulled into the driveway of Chief Wyatt's home. Robin had the table set with her best china and platters of heaping food. Ashton's headache slowly lifted as she consumed her breakfast of scrambled eggs, pancakes, and fresh-squeezed orange juice. She sat quietly at the table, watching Sawyer and her dad discussing football, marveling at how much her life had changed in such a short time.

I need to thank Allyson for allowing Grace and me the opportunity to reopen The Ramblin' Rose. If it weren't for her, I wouldn't be sitting here—with my family or with Sawyer.

After breakfast, Sawyer fetched her coat and held it for her as she slipped her arms into it, showing his eagerness to bring her back home. Grace had already left to meet a friend at church. Her parents walked them out to the truck to say goodbye. On their way down to the vehicle, Ashton stopped short and dug through her purse. "Sawyer, I can't find my phone."

He leaned against the door of the truck and folded his arms. "So, what's new?"

Ashton looked toward the house. "Mom, I think it's on your writing desk. I had to charge it so I used your cord. I'll be right back."

Sawyer pushed himself away from the vehicle. "I'll go with you."

"Hey," she said with a laugh. "I'm just going into the house. Don't worry, I'll be right back."

She ran up the stairs and headed into the kitchen. Her phone lay on the desk hooked to the charger, right where she said it would be. She pulled it off and dropped it into her purse. On her way out, she stopped, distracted by the family dog, Muffy, barking furiously in the backyard. Looking out the kitchen window, she could see the little white terrier-poodle mix reacting to something, but she couldn't see what it was.

"Muffy! Muffy! Come in the house!" She opened the door and stuck out her head to get the dog's attention, but Muffy still wouldn't quit barking. The dog must have cornered a squirrel or a neighboring cat.

"Crazy dog," she muttered as she shut the door and turned around. A solitary figure stepped into the kitchen and blocked her way.

"I knew if I waited long enough, I'd get you alone."

Before she had a chance to react to the voice, a pair of large hands clamped over her mouth and dragged her out of the house.

****

Sawyer waited impatiently for Ashton for five minutes. When she didn't come back, he started after her, but Robin insisted she go into the house to help Aston find her phone. Within a minute she reappeared.

"She's not here," Robin said frantically, standing in the front doorway. "I've looked all over the house and I can't find her!"

A chill shot down his spine. *She had to be here.* Where could she have gone?

He swiftly followed Chief Wyatt into the house and together, they searched all of the rooms. They met back in the kitchen and searched the deck.

"Look," Chief Wyatt said as he pointed toward the snowy ground by the bushes. "It looks like someone had a scuffle."

They followed the tracks to the road on the other side of the woods, where they found tire marks from a car, but nothing else. When they returned, they found Ashton's phone nearly buried in the snow.

Robin began to cry.

Trying to stay calm, Sawyer concentrated on comforting Robin by giving her an encouraging hug. Inside, however, his soul was quaking with fear. "We'll get her back," he said gently. "I promise you." He pulled out his keys. "I'm going back to her cabin to see if I can find anything there—footsteps, similar tire tracks, anything."

"Don't do anything foolish," Chief Wyatt barked at Sawyer as he made a call to the station. "I'll handle this."

Sawyer whistled to Lucy and made a beeline to his truck. He knew the chief wouldn't divulge any evidence or allow him to help so he had to do this his way. As he backed out and tore down the road, his heart twisted. He didn't need a forensic team to tell him what had happened. Cole Jacobson had waited in the woods then lurked around the deck until the opportune time and when he saw Ashton through the kitchen window, he'd brazenly abducted her.

Sawyer drove toward Ashton's cabin, growing more agitated

with each mile. How could this happen right under their noses? Why did it happen? He stared at the road ahead, coming to grips with the truth. It had nothing to do with Ashton. She, like Brenda, was an innocent pawn in a life-long game of rivalry between him and Cole.

Cole had everything money could buy in high school and he'd also had his pick of the prettiest girls around, but he went after Brenda, pursuing her until she fell for him. Now that Ashton had returned to West Loon Bay and had become involved with Sawyer, Cole suddenly wanted her back. No, he desperately wanted her back, even if it meant committing a felony to achieve it.

"Where would he go?" Sawyer said aloud to himself. "Maybe I should be asking myself—where would I go if I wanted to—to hide a person?"

The thought made him shudder. "It's not just a person, it's Ashton!" The woman he loved. The woman he had to find—alive.

He wished he knew what thoughts were going through Cole's mind. It would help lead him to where Cole had taken Ashton. One thing he *did* know.

Time was running out.

He drove around all day, mulling over the mind of Cole Jacobson, trying to second guess the man as he burned up one tank of gas after another, looking for places where Cole might have taken her. He knew Cole wouldn't take her to the resort. Chief Wyatt probably had his people crawling all over that place by now. There were dozens of private cabins in the area, but the cops would be checking out all of those, too.

No, it had to be something totally off the wall. Something no one would suspect.

He checked the railroad yards, drove around through all of the parklands, the city dump, and the trailer park. No one had seen Cole or his Mercedes.

Later that afternoon, Sawyer received a call from Chief Wyatt. They had found Cole's Mercedes abandoned in The Ramblin' Rose parking lot. He drove there and scoured the parking lot, but found nothing.

Discouraged, he went to the café to order dinner, though he didn't know if he could actually eat anything right now.

I told Ashton I'd always be there for her. I said I'd never let her down, he thought dismally as he sat down in the booth and covered his face with his hands. His heart ached for her.

I should have never let her out of my sight.

Exhausted, he tipped his head back and closed his eyes. If anything happened to her, he didn't know how he could live with it. Life wouldn't be worth living—at all.

A couple of men slid into the booth behind him, laughing and talking loudly, making him wonder if they'd just come from happy hour at The Ramblin' Rose.

"Got your fishin' gear ready, Jake?" the guy directly behind him asked.

"Yeah," Jake replied with a grunt. "Wish I could use it. That ice just ain't thick enough on the lake yet to park my fish house."

One of the men laughed. "Well, there's a few idiots already takin' a chance out there."

"Yer kiddin' me!" Jake exclaimed. "What kind of a fool would pull a fish house out on the lake now?"

"Someone who's either so stupid he doesn't know better or someone who doesn't care if the darn thing falls through."

Sawyer froze. He hadn't looked for fish houses on Lake Tremolo for the very reason Jake's dinner mate stated—the warm fall weather had prevented the ice from thickening to a safe level to hold the weight.

He tossed his menu on the table and left the restaurant, almost running to his truck. Cole knew better—he'd grown up on a resort. But did he care? That fact remained to be seen.

He tore out of the café parking lot and headed down Main Street, past the beach to the public boat landing, and looked out across the lake. Sure enough, a couple of ragtag fish houses sat like a small, abandoned village several hundred yards from the shore. He reached into his toolbox for a flashlight and a crowbar.

He and Lucy set off across the lake on foot. The full moon provided enough light to guide their way.

****

Ashton thrashed on the makeshift cot in the dark, windowless hut. Though she had on thermal boots and mittens, her hands and feet had been bound with wide tape and they were so cold she could hardly bear it. Cole had tied a cloth tightly around her mouth to keep her from crying out, but that didn't keep her from crying on the inside. Tears spilled from her eyes, dripping across her nose and onto the cot.

How could he do this to me? What kind of man could drag me out here and leave me to die in the cold? The same kind of man who held his wife in contempt for her addiction.

Cole had a cold, narcissistic heart, but he disguised it with his good looks and game show host demeanor. Inside, he cared only about number one—Cole Jacobson.

She barely knew what was happening this morning when he'd clapped his hands around her mouth and dragged her into the woods. By the time Sawyer figured out she'd disappeared, she was probably already bound and lying in the trunk of Cole's car; on the way to her unfortunate fate. At some point, the car had driven into a heated building and he'd moved her to another smaller vehicle—his Wolverine—in the dark, of course. Eventually, she'd landed here in this freezing, windowless tomb. To die all alone.

She thought about what her parents were going through right now, waiting for her to come home. Scenes of her past flashed through her mind and suddenly she regretted every rebellious act she'd ever committed in high school to defy them. It made her realize how it would feel to have a child who'd acted that way. New tears seeped from her eyes.

I want my mom...

She wondered about Sawyer. He must be frantic with worry and it hurt her to know his heart would soon be broken. Their lives had just begun. She loved him so much! At least she'd found true love, if only for a brief moment. The song he'd had the band play for her on opening night at The Ramblin' Rose kept running continuously through her head. She remembered how he'd wrapped his strong arms around her and slow-danced with her, gazing into her eyes as though they were the only two people in the room.

At least I can die knowing he loved me.

She drifted into a state of semi-consciousness, hearing distant sounds but not able to distinguish one from another. Until...

Footsteps crunched on the snow outside the building. She jerked awake, her muscles tensing as she lay in fear of Cole returning to inflict more pain on her. Strangely, the tempo of that stride sounded familiar, though she couldn't make out whose feet had passed her by.

Minutes later, the footsteps were back and by then she'd recognized another sound—a dog whining and barking.

"What's the matter, girl? Whatcha got?"

Sawyer?

Her eyes opened wide, even though she couldn't see the wall in front of her face.

Is this an illusion or am I truly hearing his voice?

She began to cry out through her gag, making any noise she could to alert him. Rolling on her stomach, she pulled her knees under her and raised herself, only to lose her balance and fall against the wall. She lay on her cot, exhausted and dizzy.

An explosion startled her. The small building began to shake. Someone was furiously pounding on the exterior with a force that frightened her, ripping pieces of the siding off in rapid succession.

Suddenly, a hole appeared in the hut and the moon shone through, but with it came a blast of cold air. A light shined on her face, blinding her. Another explosion of force with pieces flying rocked the hut, making the hole much larger.

Did someone call my name?

Warm, shaking hands removed her gag then cut off the bands on her hands and feet. Strong arms lifted her and held her close.

Is someone crying? I wonder why...

Bright lights flooded the hut. Loud, agitated voices echoed through the dark.

Then the ice began to crack.

Chapter 10

Twenty-four hours later…

Ashton slowly opened her eyes but didn't have the strength to move.

Where am I?

Someone sat next to her bed, holding her hand. The moment she stirred, he stood up and leaned over her. His smile trembled. Tears of joy pooled in his eyes—green—like hers.

"Dad?" The word came out sounding like a hoarse croak.

"Sh-h-h." He rubbed her palm with his thumbs. "Just rest. I'll still be here when you wake up."

She'd never seen her father cry before and didn't know what to make of it. "What's wrong?"

"Nothing, sweetheart," he said quietly as he patted her hand. "You're going to be just fine."

Okay…

She closed her eyes. "Where am I?" she whispered. "What happened?"

He hesitated. "You're in the hospital. Now just rest. We can talk about it later."

"But…where is everybody," she persisted and tried to lift her head. "Where's Mom and Grace?"

"They went to the cafeteria to get some coffee and toast, but they'll be back soon."

She nodded and gave him a weak smile. Though he didn't say the words, the tenderness in his manner told her how much he loved her. Growing up, he'd never spoken of his feelings for her, but that didn't matter now. His love for her shone through his doting expression, softening the hard lines of his face.

She sighed and closed her eyes again in confusion. Something lurked in the back of her mind, something important, but what was it? Her mind was tired, her thoughts were hazy. She drifted off to sleep again.

Suddenly, the sound of a door opening awoke her and someone entered the small, dim room. The muffled sound of his tennis shoes crossing the tile floor sounded comfortingly familiar. *His* footsteps? How did she know it was a man...

"Here's your coffee," the man whispered. "How is she doing? Any change?"

That voice. She knew that voice, but who—

"Thanks, Sawyer," her father whispered in response. "She woke up briefly but went back to sleep. How much do I owe you?"

Suddenly it all came flooding back to her; the cramped trunk, the dark fish house, and the tears of defeat she'd shed on a cold, lonely night.

Her eyes flew open. "Sawyer?" she whispered and lifted her head as she tried to sit up. "Is that you?"

He nearly dropped the steaming cup of coffee he held when he started at the sound of her voice, but he managed to set it down and lean over the bed. "Ashton," he said gently as he lowered her back down with shaking hands. Dark circles underscored his eyes. Exhaustion threaded his deep voice. "Take it easy. You're still pretty weak."

"I want to go home, Sawyer." Her voice started to break. "Take me home."

He leaned over and kissed her lightly on the lips. "You need to get well first, but I will when the doctor says you can go."

Cole's face flashed in her mind and she shivered. "Promise?"

He nodded. "Just close your eyes now and go back to sleep. I won't leave you. I've been here all along." He leaned closer and whispered in her ear, "We'll never be separated ever again. This I promise you."

Epilogue

December 25th

"Oh, my gosh! Look what Travis gave me!"

Ashton smiled at her sister's excitement as Grace held up a shiny red satin box containing a fat, wriggling puppy with short curly hair. The "friendly" date she and Travis had made to discuss a well-done cheeseburger had turned into a "steady" date arrangement, including the get-together today.

Rose, Ruth, and Robin had organized a holiday family reunion at The Ramblin' Rose for Christmas Day with a potluck buffet and plenty of sugary desserts. The sisters had hosted the event for the entire extended family to come together and celebrate Ashton's full recovery from hypothermia. Her abduction and near-death disaster had shaken the family, bringing everyone closer together.

No one, though, had come through the event growing closer to Ashton than Sawyer.

"Have I told you today how much I love you?" His arm possessively cuddled her as they nestled into one of the new corner booths.

Ashton chuckled. "Only a dozen times. You have my permission to say it again."

He quietly murmured in her ear. "I love you."

They had been inseparable since the night he'd pulled her from the small fish house on Lake Tremolo. The only thing that saved her was finding her in time and getting her transported to the hospital to begin the slow process of warming her body.

Cole had not fared as well. He'd seen the flashlight beam on the lake as Sawyer ripped the fish house apart. In anger, Cole had foolishly driven his Wolverine across the ice to punish Sawyer and reclaim Ashton. He'd escaped the vehicle before the ice collapsed underneath it and sunk it, but he hadn't scrambled far enough away. The ice shelf broke under his feet and plunged him into the lake.

News of Cole's death had hit Brenda so hard she'd become hysteric and had to be hospitalized. Though she and Brenda would never be friends, Ashton couldn't help feeling empathy for the fragile woman, losing her husband the way she did. His funeral had been one of the largest ever held in West Loon Bay. Since then, Brenda's family had convinced her to enter a treatment program for her opioid addiction. Hopefully, she would now get the help she needed.

Since Ashton's abduction and hospitalization, The Ramblin' Rose's business had steadily increased to the point of needing to hire workers. At first, most of the people who came into the bar were curious to know about Ashton's condition and how her recovery was coming along, but once they visited the place, they began coming back.

"Come on." Sawyer stood up and handed Ashton her new down-filled coat with a fur-lined hood, one of his Christmas gifts to her. "We need to find a place where it's quiet so we can talk—alone."

She wrapped her red scarf around her neck and slid her arms into the warmest coat she had ever owned.

Allyson stood by the door, wearing a proud grin. "See? I knew you two would end up together."

Ashton stopped with her hand on the door and gave her cousin a wry smile. "What did you do, check your crystal ball?"

Allyson's blue eyes twinkled as she smiled mischievously, looking pretty much like she did the day they'd decided to form a team and open The Ramblin' Rose. "For your information, I'm the one who hired Sawyer to remodel this place. I knew as soon as you two got into the same room, sparks would fly."

Ashton opened her mouth to slam a comeback at her, but Sawyer came between them, covering their mouths with each of his hands. "Time out. You two can mud-wrestle when we come back."

"Mud-wrestle!" They said in unison and began to laugh.

Sawyer opened the door and pulled Ashton outside to get her away from the crowd. Light snow had begun to fall, making a soft whispering sound in the still night air. Large, sticky snowflakes clung to the pine garland, and red bows fastened to the turn-of-the-century streetlights. They walked along the deserted, brightly lit sidewalk without talking, just enjoying being together.

At the corner, Sawyer stopped under the streetlight and pulled a pearly white box from his coat pocket.

"What's that?" Ashton asked as he held it out to her.

"For you. Another little Christmas present."

"Oh," she said excitedly and pulled off her mittens to open the box. Inside she found an ornament; a white porcelain heart rimmed in gold with hand-painted gold flowers and garnished with two rings looped with white ribbon under a small bow. "This is so pretty." She lifted on her tiptoes and kissed him. "I'll hang it on the tree tonight."

"Well, I think you'd better take another look at it and this time, examine it a little closer."

"What?" She held it up to the light. "What am I supp—" She blinked in surprise. "Are these rings the real thing?"

He gazed down at her with a teasing grin. "They might be. Why don't you try them on?"

She untied the bow and slipped on the engagement ring of yellow gold and a heart-shaped diamond. "It's a perfect fit! Sawyer, how did you know my size?"

He grinned. "Your mother might have had a little something to do with it."

Her mother, Ashton had learned, might have had *a little*

something to do with a lot of things lately. Aunt Rose had visited her at the hospital and confessed that turning the bar over to Allyson, Grace, and Ashton had been Robin's idea. Robin had even offered to come up with half of the business loan for the girls. She so desperately wanted both of her daughters to move back home that she'd concocted the scheme all by herself. Aunt Rose had liked the idea so much she'd agreed to team up with Robin and keep her as a silent partner. No wonder Bob hadn't been happy about it, or able to change Aunt Rose's mind.

Sawyer lowered his head, the tip of his nose brushing hers. "Will you marry me, Ashton Wyatt?"

"Yes," she said happily clutching the little white box. "Thank you for the most wonderful Christmas gift of all, Sawyer. *Your love.*"

The End (for now...)

The story continues when Allyson and Grace each get their own books— coming soon!

If you enjoyed *Once Upon a Christmas*, please post a review on Amazon at https://www.amazon.com/dp/B07H1RXV1X. Thank you!

~*~

Enjoy this sneak peek of another Christmas story by Denise Devine!

A Christmas to Remember

Chapter One

The winter storm started as a steady drizzle as Katie McGowan left Fargo on I-94 East, heading back to Minneapolis. She'd spent the last four days in Fargo, North Dakota, at the new branch office of Prairie Star Newspapers, reviewing the benefits package with each employee and completing the paperwork. On Friday morning, she'd left early to get ahead of the storm, but it quickly caught up with her.

"Why do we have to get bad weather on the same day I'm driving back to Minneapolis?" Katie complained aloud, her heart pounding like a jackhammer as she peered through the flapping windshield wipers. "This had better not mess up my holiday!"

She'd planned to spend the weekend with her parents and get into the Christmas mood by watching classic holiday movies and helping her mom bake fancy cookies. Mom and Dad were expecting her for dinner tonight at six o'clock, but the way things looked now, she might not make it back to Minneapolis until very late.

Oh, well, she thought, *I'll catch up on sleep after Christmas.*

As blustery Canadian winds pushed into Minnesota, the drizzle turned to sleet then became a rippling curtain of solid white, limiting her visibility to the taillights on the vehicle ahead. Slippery conditions and blowing snow forced her to reduce her speed to forty miles per hour. At thirty-three, Katie considered herself a pretty good driver in bad weather, but she'd never experienced anything like *this*.

The Malibu began to slide toward the shoulder, as though being pushed by an invisible force. Snow scraped the underside of her car, causing her to grip the wheel with white-knuckled hands. Slowly, she straightened the front wheels and steered back into the grooves carved by the huge tires of the monstrous pickup truck ahead of her.

Buried deep in her purse, her phone began to ring, but she let it go to voicemail and concentrated on her driving. She couldn't even glance away from the road much less reach across the seat and dig into her bag.

Through the blowing snow, Katie spied a large green sign that read "Alexandria, Exit 100" and let out a small cheer. Luckily, the truck ahead of her drove up the exit first and plowed a path for her. At the top of the ramp, she stared through the swirling white cloud, wondering which way to go. Though she knew the city of Alexandria well, the whiteout conditions disoriented her, causing her to lose all sense of direction. She desperately needed to find a gas station where she could pull in temporarily and call home.

At the top of the exit, the truck turned right. She glanced around, surveying her limited options. To her left, the road looked impassable, covered with at least a foot of snow. She decided to play it safe and follow the truck.

Straight ahead, Katie saw a snowplowing contractor clearing the parking lot of a large gas station. Breathing a sigh of relief, she veered her car onto the frontage road and drove to the station.

Her phone began ringing again. She parked under the shelter of the station's canopy and tore through her purse. The caller ID displayed *Prairie Star Newspapers*. "Hello?"

"Katie, where are you? I've been trying to reach you for over an hour! Are you okay?"

"I've got a major case of the shakes, but otherwise, I'm fine," she said to Marcey, the Executive Assistant to the Director of Human Resources at the newspaper office. "I'm in Minnesota now at a gas station in Alexandria. The snow is coming down so fast I can hardly see to drive, much less answer calls. How's the weather in Minneapolis?"

"I'm so glad you're all right! It's starting to sleet here and the snow isn't far behind," Marcey said. "According to the weatherman, MNDOT is closing down I-94 at Alexandria because the wind is creating impossible driving conditions. You escaped just in time. The barricades are going up right now and the Highway Patrol is directing people off the freeway. You'll have to spend the night there, but don't worry, I'm searching the Internet right now for a hotel room for you."

Katie gripped the phone. Spend the night here? No way! "Marcey, I can't stay in Alexandria tonight. Tomorrow is Christmas Eve! Mom and Dad are expecting me for dinner and I have to stop at my apartment first to pick up gifts."

"Hold on," Marcey said, ignoring her plea. Marcey went silent except for the clickety click of her typing. "Katie, I have a list of accommodations for the area and I'm working my way through it. I'd better get back to calling before everything fills up. Sit tight. I'll call you back as soon as I can."

"Marcey, wait—" The line went dead.

Katie tossed her phone on the seat and stared out the window. This couldn't be happening. She had to get home tonight!

Her stomach rumbled, prompting her to dig through her bag for something to snack on. She'd missed lunch an hour ago, so a Snickers bar and a half-empty bag of strawberry Twizzlers would have to do. She bit into a Twizzlers stick and called her mother. No one answered. She tried her father's cell phone. That rang repeatedly, too.

"Where are they?" she said aloud in frustration, chewing on a mouthful of candy. Her parents had a bad habit of forgetting their cell phones at home or simply not hearing the phones ring if they were watching the news. Over the years, her father had gradually lost his hearing in one ear, but rather than wear a hearing aid, he preferred to crank up the volume instead. They were probably sitting in front of the

TV right now, getting the latest updates on the weather, and wondering why she hadn't called.

The call went to voicemail. "Hi, Dad," she said, "this is the first chance I've had to check my missed calls this morning. Don't worry. I'm okay. I made it as far as Alexandria, but it looks like I'm stuck here overnight because the Highway Patrol is closing down the freeway. My boss' assistant is booking a room for me right now. Tell Mom I'm sorry I can't make it for dinner. I'll call her when I reach the hotel. Bye."

Katie disconnected the call and sat staring at the snow dancing across her windshield in swirling gusts. She didn't want to stay here overnight. She didn't want to be stuck in this town! Reaching into her bag, she pulled out the Snickers bar. When upset, eat chocolate!

I need to get back on that freeway and be on my way.

A couple of minutes later, Marcey rang her back.

"I've got good news and bad news," Marcey said. "Which one do you want first?"

"I could use some good news about now."

"Right! The good news is, I found you a first-rate hotel and the only rooms left were the king suites, so you're going to spend the night getting the royal treatment."

"What's so bad about that?" Katie stuffed the last bite of the Snickers bar in her mouth.

She heard Marcey draw in a deep breath. "...it's at Lakewood Resort."

The candy bar stuck in her throat like a glob of sugary cement. She swallowed hard. "I *can't* stay there. You know that. Please find me something else."

"Believe me, I would if I could," Marcey said, her voice threaded with regret. "I'm so sorry, Katie, but that's the only hotel left with anything available in the entire city. All of the less expensive accommodations went first and the others filled up after that. There were only two suites left at the resort when I called and the other one is most likely gone by now, too."

Katie's heart began to slam in her chest. "I-I can't do this. You know that's where...where Josh..."

The scene came back with startling clarity; the grinding howl of snowmobile engines, the explosive crash of metal on metal, the screams...Josh airborne then his lifeless body crumpled in the snow...

"I know it's hard to go back to the place where Josh was...had his accident, Katie, but you have no other choice."

"I have an emergency kit in my trunk. I could pull into another hotel parking lot and keep the car running to stay warm."

"Katie, that's unthinkable! What will you do to keep warm once the gas runs out? And that's not your only problem."

Distracted by the crash scene blaring in her head, Katie barely heard Marcey's words. "What do you mean?"

"What will you do when you have to use the bathroom?"

The words "use the bathroom" forced her to focus. It would be tough to sit in a cold car with no food, watching the snow pile up as her only entertainment, but the thought of not having any "facilities," as her dad would say, gave her pause. A hot shower and something good to eat sounded wonderful right now, just not at Lakewood Resort!

"You *can* do this, Katie. It's been two years since you've last seen the place." Marcey paused as if to give her a chance to think it over. "Maybe going back there is just what you need."

Though Marcey would never be tactless enough to say the words, the implication of what she really meant came across loud and clear. *Going back to Lakewood Resort will force you to face Josh's death, finally, and move on with your life.*

No way, Katie thought stubbornly. She'd vowed never to come back to Lakewood Resort because it had caused her too much pain. *I don't want to deal with that now—or ever.*

A sudden gust of wind rocked the Malibu. She checked the gas gauge. The needle pointed to the halfway mark. One-half of a tank would not last long. She could brave the storm and fill up here, but even a full tank wouldn't get her through the night. She stared across the parking lot, knowing she had to get going and the longer she procrastinated, the worse it would be once she got back on the road. The area the snowplow had cleared already had an accumulation of new snow.

Katie let out a deep breath. "Marcey, are you still there?"

"Of course I am. I'm not hanging up until you promise me that you're going to take that room at the Lakewood Resort and be safe."

She went silent for a few moments, mulling it over. "This is *not* fair," she said in a grumbling voice. "I'll drive over there and give it a try, but I'm not guaranteeing I'll stay."

"Wonderful! Do you need directions?"

"No. I'll use my cell phone GPS."

"Great! Look, I have the weather report on my monitor and you need to leave *now*. This storm is turning into a slow-moving blizzard and the longer you wait, the more dangerous it's becoming. Get going before the police have to form a search party to find you."

"Okay," Katie said, becoming alarmed at the prospect of getting lost or worse, ending up in the ditch. "The Lakewood Resort can't be far from here, but I have no idea what condition the roads are in over there by Lake Darling."

"Drive carefully and call me as soon as you arrive. If I don't hear from you in twenty minutes, I'm going to call 9-1-1!"

Katie hung up and got busy pulling up the directions on her phone. As soon as she drove out of the lot and turned onto the main road, her car began to slide, but she reduced her speed and kept moving. She drove toward the freeway and risked a glance as she passed the northbound on-ramp, hoping the Highway Patrol hadn't closed the barrier yet.

She gasped when she saw red and blue flashing lights from a half-dozen squad cars on the freeway below. It looked like a semi-truck and trailer had jackknifed across the southbound lanes. Vehicles filled both sides of the ditch like piles of snow-covered dominoes. Headlights beamed like beacons through the blowing snow from cars lined up waiting to be detoured onto the exit ramp once the tow trucks had cleared through the drifts to open a temporary lane. Frightened, she focused straight ahead and kept on going, passing a roadblock of police cars closing off the southbound entrance to the freeway.

The GPS led her across town, directing her turn by turn until she reached Lakewood Lane, but she couldn't let her guard down until she drove through the guest parking lot into the circular entrance at the Lakewood Resort and Conference Center.

Her stomach fluttered with dread. The last time she had stayed here, she'd departed in an ambulance with Josh and never returned. She'd buried him a few days later, exactly two weeks before Christmas. Thankfully, she'd had the love and support of her parents to help her get through the holiday that year and every year since. She couldn't imagine spending Christmas without them.

She slid to a stop under the Porte cochére and stared at the massive brick and stucco building. Pine boughs, red velvet ribbon, and multi-colored lights dressed the large windows spanning the front. A pair of snow-covered wreaths hung on the double doors of the entrance. The bell captain came out to greet her, dressed in a black jacket and fur cap. A gust of icy wind and snow swirled around her as she lowered the window, causing her to shiver.

"We're fully booked, Ma'am, but due to the blizzard, we're allowing people to take shelter in the lobby. Do you have a reservation?" The nametag on his jacket read "Ron."

"Yes, I do," Katie shouted, squinting to avoid getting snow in her eyes.

"May I assist with your luggage?"

She pressed the trunk release. "I have one bag."

"Just give the bell desk a call when you get into your room and we'll deliver it." Ron handed her a ticket for the suitcase and pointed toward the guest parking lot. "You'll have to find a spot in the open area, I'm afraid. Valet parking is full."

She raised the window and waited for him to remove her bag then stepped on the gas. But the car didn't move forward. Instead, the front wheels spun on a patch of ice, making a loud whining noise. Then the car simply slid sideways.

Ron reappeared at her window. "The valet can give you a push. Unfortunately, I only have one on duty today and he's busy helping someone else right now, so you'll have to wait your turn. When he comes back, I'll have him assist you."

A horn blast forced her to turn around and look through the back window. Several cars had lined up behind her, waiting for her to drive on so they could drop off passengers and bags under the shelter of the canopy. The guy behind her made a rude gesture and laid on his horn again.

Katie leaned her forehead against the steering wheel and groaned. Could this day get any worse?

(End of Excerpt)

Want more? Read the first chapter of this book and each of my novels on my blog at: https://www.deniseannette.blogspot.com

If you'd like to know more about me or my other books, you can visit my website at: https://www.deniseannettedevine.com

Sign up for my newsletter at http://eepurl.com/csOJZL and receive a free romantic suspense novella!

Like my Facebook page at:
https://www.facebook.com/deniseannettedevine

More Books by Denise Devine

Christmas Stories
Merry Christmas, Darling
A Christmas to Remember
A Merry Little Christmas
Once Upon a Christmas
A Very Merry Christmas - Hawaiian Holiday Series
~*~

Bride Books
The Encore Bride
Lisa – Beach Brides Series
Ava – Perfect Match Series
~*~

Moonshine Madness Series – Historical Suspense/Romance
The Bootlegger's Wife – Book 1
Guarding the Bootlegger's Widow – Book 2
The Bootlegger's Legacy – Book 3 - Coming Fall 2021
~*~

West Loon Bay Series – Small Town Romance
Small Town Girl – Book 1
Brown-Eyed Girl – Book 2 (Coming Soon)
~*~

Unfinished Business – A Cozy Mystery

Dark Fortune – A Cozy Mystery
This Time Forever - an inspirational romance
Romance and Mystery Under the Northern Lights – short stories
Northern Intrigue – an anthology of mystery stories
Recipes of Love (cookbook)

Want more? Read the first chapter of each of Denise's most popular novels on her blog at:
https://deniseannette.blogspot.com